A Day's Notice

Written by Paris Keal

To Believe or Not Believe ...

A Day's Notice

Paris Keal

a novel

First edition. 2020

ISBN: 978-0-578-66694-5

LCCN: 2020905486

For my family and friends who have provided

me with overwhelming love and support to share this message

that was placed on my heart.

To anyone in this world that I've ever come across that spoke life
into me and my dreams.

Authors Note

I wrote this story in twenty four days during National Novel Writing Month in November of 2019. With no writing experience I made the decision to tell this story that was heavy on my heart. This may not be the most profound piece of literature, but it has a valid meaning. I wrote this novel to remind people that tomorrow is not promised. We as individuals put things and people off until tomorrow carelessly looking over the fact that tomorrow may never come. While editing this book I saw on Twitter the news about Kobe Bryant and it shook me to my core. With people as influential as he was you always assume we will lose them to old age. Since the beginning of writing this book the phrase "Live Life For Today" has been weighing in the back on my mind and with his tragic death it only amplified that. If you don't take anything away from this book at least remember to treat today like it's your last time to get it right because it just might be.

Donathan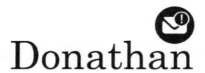

I jump out of my sleep in a cold sweat. The nightmare I was having felt so real to me. The tears, the gut-wrenching pain, and breathlessness in my chest seemed to consume me. When I look over at the clock, I realize it's only eight in the morning. Great, sleeping in is out of the question now. I hate that I'm such a workaholic, my body won't let me relax.

I glance over at my stunning girlfriend, Vorie, and she's still sound asleep. I ease out of bed with care and make my way to the bathroom. As I take a seat, I unplug my phone from the charger and do the regular social media check. Starting with Twitter, I scroll down my timeline a little bit. Usually it's not as active this early, so I then move onto Instagram, and see what I've missed from the night before. After giving a couple likes, I carry onto Snapchat, and see what videos people have posted recently. None of my feeds are interesting right now, so I put my phone

1

back down on the bathroom counter, flush, and get up to wash my hands.

Heading to the kitchen to get a quick drink, I see she's left me a note that we need to go to the grocery store today. Annoyed I can't have my regular morning glass of orange juice, I fill my glass with water from the fridge. I take my unsatisfying water back to bed and lay down.

Staring at the ceiling, I think about my nightmare again. I know it's said that dreams and nightmares are projections of the subconscious mind, but I pray that's a myth. Reaching under the bed I take out my laptop. While I'm up I should check some emails.

I open my work email and as expected there are plenty of messages that need responding. As I'm replying to important messages, I see a topic line that catches my eye. I don't know who's emailing people from itsmejesus2@heavenlyworks.com but it's clearly a joke. For kicks and giggles I open the email:

From: itsmejesus2@heavenlyworks.com
To: EVERYONE
Date: November 7th, 2020, 7:00 a.m.
Subject: IT'S ME JESUS, ITS URGENT!

To my siblings,

Yes, it's me.

No, this is not a joke.

Please read the following message through and through:

Dad's pissed! He's been overseeing what's been going on down there for some time now, and he's not happy. He's tried everything he could do to keep you guys on the right track, but you all keep ignoring his signs. I tried to talk him out of what he wants to do. I tried to get him to send me back down there, but he says we've already done that before. I tried to do my part as your big brother to look out for you, but you guys have gone and pissed the big man off. Long story short he's shutting everything down tomorrow. I talked him into giving everyone 24 hours to have on earth to tie up

3

any loose ends they may have. Take this time to spend with family, be adventurous, or pray. I'm sorry about this but we have a lot of reconstructing we have to do, and we can't do it with you all there.

Please know that this is not a drill but the real deal.

I'll see you tomorrow.........hopefully.

P.S. – Whoever is using the original itsmejesus@heavenlyworks.com we need to talk.

Sincerely your brother,

J. C.

I read this email three times. I closed my laptop, opened it, restarted it, and read the message again. On one hand I'm confused but then again I also want to laugh. This is some sort of sick joke some loser is pulling on me. I check the email again and start to wonder how they even got my work email. This has to be one of my employees or previous clients because they're the only ones with it. Setting my laptop down, I race back to my phone I left on the bathroom counter.

My fingers are already taking me to my personal email app before my brain can process what I'm doing. I close my eyes and tell myself it won't be there. Loosening my grip on the phone, I take a couple deep breaths before building the courage to look at my screen. When my eyes open, they shoot to the first message that appears at the top of the screen. My stomach drops to my feet, and my chest tightens.
Opening the email, I read the same words again for the fifth time. Now, I start to get upset

because not only is this prick playing with my personal email, but also with my work one. As I stare at my screen, I know this can't be real. Can it? I mean Jesus wouldn't send us an email. Can he send us emails? No, no, no! Clearly he can't, and I'm having a momentary lapse in judgement. He doesn't even have electronics up there, right? How would he even...I stop. I take a breath and sit down. There is no way that this is real.

I'm staring at my phone in disbelief with no idea what to do with this information. If this little email is real, then I couldn't have been the only person to get it. I go to Twitter and see what's trending in the world. The first hashtag says #Jesusemail. Deep down, I'm praying that this means something else. I click it. There are endless posts about this email. I'm so happy that I used the bathroom before I checked my emails because my stomach is in shambles right now. I start to read the post I see under this hashtag and I can feel my heart speed up with each one.

 **KenJohns**
@kenziejohns_

This email is craxy! I don't believe it
though. Do you?
#Jesusmail

7:25 AM - 7 Nov 2020

 **RagiLynn**
@Girlragi_

Did anyone else get this creepy email from
ItsmeJesus@heavenlyworks.com ????
#Jesusmail

7:45 AM - 7 Nov 2020

 **AhryFay**
@_ahryyyy

Clearly somebody is in a joking mood.
Whoever sent that email from a Jesus
account GO TO HELL! #Jesusmail

8:00 AM - 7 Nov 2020

 **VaunRay**
@jauvanray

I got this email supposedly from Jesus and
I think it's real. Did anyone else get it?
#Jesusmail

8:07 AM - 7 Nov 2020

Reading these posts has brought on a headache and made it worse. I can't fathom what to believe right now. On the one hand this could be some sick joke but with God, anything is possible. Reaching in the medicine cabinet, I pull out two pain relievers. I take them and can't help but to open the email again. The words start to come off the screen and create a whirlwind around my brain.

What am I supposed to do in this situation? What do I do with this information? I can feel I'm going to be sick. I fall to my knees in front of the toilet, and I stick my head in the bowl. I feel all the water I drunk this morning sitting in the back of my throat. As I'm on the floor, my ears single in on the ticking of my clock sitting on my bedside table. Each moment I let pass is time that I'm losing, but I don't know if I believe in this yet. This decision is too big for me to make on my own. I need Vorie's opinion.

Entering the bedroom I see she's still sleeping peacefully. I can't wake her with this crap. What do I say? "Hey babe, I know you're tired, but I got an email from Jesus saying the world's going to end tomorrow. I sort of believe it, but I'm not sure, so can you see if

you got the same email and tell me what you think..."
I cannot say that. She'll think I'm crazy; maybe I
could ease this into a conversation somehow. With
care I get into bed and try to get comfortable so I can
wait until she wakes.

I lay still for at least ten seconds before I give into
myself and push her to try wake her up. Apparently, I
don't know my own strength because she flips right
onto the floor.

Vorie

I'm on the floor. I have no idea how I got
down here. Sitting up, I see Donathan looking at me.
"Did you push me on the floor?" I ask him. He shakes
his head no instantaneously. Too bad for him I know
when he's lying. "Do it again and trust me I'll push
you back," I say getting off the floor and taking a seat
on the edge of the bed. Of course, he had to interrupt
the best sleep I've had in months. I get out of bed and
make my way to the bathroom.

I sit down to relieve myself, and when I look up
Donathan is staring at me. I swear if I didn't love this
man I'd kill him. "What do you want Donathan? Is
something wrong?" I ask him. He tells me no but
keeps staring at me. I roll my eyes, get up, and wash
my hands. I'll never understand how I ended up with
such a strange man. I walk back through the room
and head to the kitchen. Taking a glass from the
cabinet I fill it with water. I yell from the kitchen,
"Don, did you see my note about the groceries?"
Turning around I see he's standing right at the end of

the kitchen island. I jump. "Jesus! Donathan, what has gotten into you this morning?" I ask him. He's acting all suspicious and I can see clear as day that he's trying to hide something from me.

"Yes, I saw your note," he says in a shaky voice. As I'm drinking from my glass, I notice his body language. He's gripping the kitchen island so hard his knuckles are white. His forehead is sweating, and his breathing is fast. "Baby tell me what's wrong; I can see it all over your body that something is bothering you," I say. He walks from the island to the couch and tells me to come sit next to him. I walk over and sit down.

"Earlier this morning I got an email. I know you're going to think I'm crazy, but hear me out before you respond," he tells me. I agree but I'm already skeptical of what he's about to say. "An email addressed from Jesus came to me this morning. It claims that the world will be ending tomorrow," he finished. Before I can give him a response laughter begins to flood out my mouth. I'm laughing so hard that I can feel my sides begin to tense up. This man sitting in front of me must be joking. He's not laughing with me, but I know he's trying to pull a prank on me. "Donathan come on, stop playing so much. Today is one of our only days off together. I actually wanted to get out of the apartment to spend time together, not joke around like this," I tell him. He's still staring at me with a straight face and this is starting to feel less like a game.

"Vorie, I'm not joking with you right now. Go get your phone," he tells me. To humor him, I get up and walk back into the bedroom. Taking my phone off the charger, I bring it back in the living room to him. He takes it from me, unlocks it, and goes straight to my emails. "What is your most recent email?" he asks as he's handing my phone back to me. I don't want to, but I take the phone and look down. To my surprise there is an email from a itsmeJesus2@heavenly-works.com. I'm shocked, but this still must be a part of his little joke. He tells me to read it and I do. I don't know what to make of this email. Looking up, Donathan is staring at me again. I can tell from the look in his eyes that he's frightened. "What is this?" I ask. He explains to me that the email was in his work email, personal email, and all-over social media. I go on Twitter, and I see that people all down my timeline are talking about it. Some believe, others are choosing to ignore, and the majority are confused about what is going on. I inquire does he believe in this absurd email and starts to pace the living room in front of me. "Honestly, I have no idea what to believe that's why I woke you," he tells me.

I sit in our living room frozen on the couch in fear. I am a believer and a firm one at that, yet, I cannot fathom the idea of this being anywhere near true. If this is a joke, this is a sick one to play on people, but who could have the power to make this so widespread. What are we going to do?

He woke me up thinking I would have all the answers, and I'm just as confused if not more than he is. He comes back and sits next to me on the couch. We're staring off into the oblivion with no answer for one another. Do we believe this email and try to make the best out the time that we have left? Do we keep living and take a chance ignoring this? "I believe," I declare. He looks at me like I have two heads. "Are you sure Vorie?" he asks me. I announce I'd rather be a fool now than be sorry later. I can tell from the look on his face that he's still unsure. "Look rather this is real or not, we can't sit in the apartment all day and ponder," I say. He looks at me, and I can tell he thinks I'm crazy. "Say I believe like you do, and we do in fact have a few hours left to spend together…what would you want to do?" he asks me.

Not immediately knowing the answer I walk to the kitchen to put my glass away and it hits me. I run to the bedroom and go straight for my purse. After moving some old receipts around I found my crumbled-up piece of paper. Taking my little ball to the front room, I toss it on Donathan's lap. He looks at me confused and I gesture for him to open it.

"What is this," he asks me. I say it's the list of things we've wanted to do but have been holding out on. We thought we'd have a lifetime to check everything off. "Let's try to do everything on our *Together Let's List*. Regardless if the email is real or not, we can spend the day making memories. It could be the best last day ever or just another Saturday. What do you say?" I ask. He looks from me to the list.

Together Let's...
1) Sky Diving
2) Picnic in the Park Lunch
3) Plan Each Other's Outfit
4) Horseback Riding
5) Paintball Gun War
6) Paint Together
7) Matching Tattoos
8) Couples Massage
9) Kiss on Top the Ferris Wheel
10) Skating
11) Go to The Club Together
12) Karaoke Night
13) Dance on The Beach
14) Expensive Dinner
15) Sleep Under The Stars

I watch him read the list and wait to see what he'll say. He looks up and I can't read his expression. Finally, he smiles and agrees to do this with me today. Regardless of what today could mean, this makes me the most excited I've been in a while. We're both very invested in our work lives. I can't remember when was the last time we went out and spent some quality time together. Hanging in the house is fun but I love going out and experiencing new things.

He suggests that we pick out each other's outfit before choosing what task on our list we're going to tackle first. Coming from the man that requests I style him for work each morning, I'm already dreading what he could pick out for me. I tell him that I'll go take a shower first and he can go pick out my outfit. I get up and make a beeline to the bathroom. I feel him grab my hand as I pass him. Spinning me around suddenly places me in his arms. He kisses me and sends a warm tingle down my spine. We stand embracing each other for what feels like forever. "Time is ticking," I say while breaking away and making it to the bathroom. Closing the door behind me, I turn the shower on piping hot. I don't know what I'm getting myself into today, but I know it won't be a boring one.

Donathan

I'm standing in the closet looking at all
this girl's clothes, and I have no idea what I'm doing.
She has rows and rows of clothes, and I'm supposed to
pick the outfit that she could die in. This is too much
pressure for one man. I go into the kitchen and reach
into my lucky cabinet. I take a shot glass and pour me
some whiskey. Oh, don't you dare judge me; this could
be my last day on earth. I take my shot and make my
way back into the closet. I want to pick something she
can be comfortable in, but I have no clue what we'll be
doing all day.

As I'm pushing things aside nothing is speaking
to me. If this is what we think it is I want today to be
special. Nothing hanging up is going to do it, so I
move onto what's in her drawers. I search drawer
after drawer, but nothing is reaching out at me. This
is exactly why she styles my work attire each day.
Getting to the bottom drawer, I take out the first shirt
she has laying on top. It's cute but not cute enough for
today. Under that shirt, I find a classic cotton brown

19

colored dress. I haven't seen this dress since the night I met Vorie two years ago. I'll never forget that night.

I walk into a bar late one afternoon. My buddies and I closed a major deal and want to treat ourselves for working so hard. We're sitting at the bar getting a round of shots when I look over and see a girl crying in the corner. I try to pay her no mind because let's be honest here this was a night of celebration with my boys. I wasn't going to ruin it trying to go speak to the girl in the corner. And I was told never approach a crier, they've got baggage. I take shot after shot with my boys and when I say we're knocking them back I mean it. I can't squeeze my legs together any longer, so I get up and go to the bathroom.

From the bathroom, I can still hear this girl crying. At this point I'm like ma'am it can NOT be healthy to cry this much. I leave the bathroom and come take a seat next to her. I don't ask her name or what's wrong I reach into my suit pocket and hand her my handkerchief. She takes it from my hand and says thank you.

After wiping her eyes, she gives it back. I tell her I can either get up and go back to celebrating or I can sit here with her and she can tell me what's going on. She looks at me with the most beautiful hazel eyes I've ever seen and asks how can I trust you. I say "Miss, no man is approaching a woman crying in the corner for thirty minutes if he wants an easy night." For the first time that night, she smiled at me. After that, I knew I'd do whatever to see her smile at me like that again. She told me some story about getting passed over for a promotion she'd been looking forward to. Don't ask me if that's exactly what she said because I was a little distracted. Yes, I'm a gentleman but I'm still a man and this woman was astronomically out of my league.

Zarek came over to tell me the guys were leaving. Looking at my watch for the first time in a long time I realized I had been sitting with this woman for an hour. He asks me if I needed a ride home and if I can be quite frank with you,

21

I had no intentions of leaving her. I tell him I'll call an Uber and make it home fine.

Now it's her and I again and my palms are sweating so much I could make a puddle on the bar counter if I wanted to. With no expectation I ask this woman to accompany me in getting a bite to eat. By the grace of God, she tells me yes. We get up to leave the bar and I haven't even thought about where I'm going to take us. Getting outside I see it's a little chilly, so I take my jacket off and put it around her shoulders.

My feet carry us to my favorite breakfast spot a couple of blocks over. Walking us in, I bring her over to my usual table. I look behind the counter and see that my buddy Camden is on shift, so I'm praying he catches my eyes so I can give him the wink. He'll know that means I need him as my wing-man to help me look good. I see him picking up two menus but he's not looking up. He's walking this way, but he never glances up, so I pray he does not mess this up for me before I even find out her name. He gets

to the table and sees me. I can tell from his
facial expression that he is going to do
something stupid. With a questionable smile, he
asks for our drink order. I hear her say
something, but my mind is only focused on him
and his next move. He looks at me and says
"And for you, sir? Would you like that same half
tea half lemonade you had on your previous
date earlier tonight?" Now that's a move I did
not expect, so I sit there in a state of shock. She's
looking at me with a look of disbelief and this
sly sucker is smiling. Before I can even fathom
an answer, he walks away. Now, I'm left to deal
with the mess he spilled in my lap.

The only thing I can utter out my mouth
is an I'm sorry. She looks at me and looks back
down at the menu. At this point, I don't know
what I'm going to say to get me out of this. Then
she says the last thing I thought she would say,
"He's your friend, isn't he?". It takes me by
surprise so all I can do is shake my head yes.
This woman tells me, "I noticed him smile at
you right when we walked in. You've been

23

staring in his direction since we sat down. If you turn around right now he's staring at us." Sure enough when I turn around this fool waves at me. I turn back to her and she's smiling at me again. She picks up her menu to where it's covering her mouth and says, "Plus how dumb would you be to bring another girl the same place you were at just hours ago?". If her smile and beautiful face didn't already attract me, her sense of humor definitely sealed the deal.

Camden comes to take her order. I get the same thing every time I come here and as often as that is he knows my order by heart. It doesn't take long for the food to come out. We eat while continuing our conversation and the more I learn about her, the more she intrigues me. Everything is going great until those shots I had earlier start flowing through me and not in a good way. I inform her I have to go to the bathroom and that I'll be right back. I move as quickly as I can, because I want to get back to her. I come out, hit the corner, and see she's gone. I assume she went to the bathroom herself.

Walking back to the table I sit down and notice the receipt. I knew I blew it man. Taking a closer look at the receipt I noticed that she paid. I flip it over and read:

Thanks for the great conversation tonight.

-Vorie

(584)749-0010

My heart jumped inside my chest. That night was the start of us.

I take the dress and set it down and our bed. I don't know if she'll remember what dress this is, but I know this is what I want to look at if it's my last day here. Thinking of the night we met makes me want to do something special for her. I walk to the kitchen and open the fridge to see if we have what I need. Just my luck the only ingredients we have are exactly what the recipe requires. If she doesn't remember where this is from I am definitely going to be pissed.

Vorie

I cut the water off and get out of the
shower. I'm feeling refreshed and clean. Drying off I
catch a glimpse of myself in the mirror. Looking at
me, I see my eyes begin to glisten. What am I doing
carrying on like today isn't possibly my last day on
earth? On one hand, what we're doing is romantic but
on the other how can we spend the day acting normal?
My mind goes to the man that's on the other side of
this apartment. Today may not be for certain but I
know my love for him is. I have to at least try to make
this day with him all about us. I have no idea how I'm
going to calm my nerves, but I have to put my best
foot forward. I wrap my towel around me and head
into the bedroom.

I'm looking around for what this man has put
out for me and I'm not seeing it. "Babe where'd you
put my outfit," I scream into the other room. He
replies that it's on the bed, but I must be blind. Nicely
folded on the edge of the bed I see a familiar brown
color. I unfold it and immediately I know where this

26

dress is from. This is the dress that I was wearing the night I met Donathan. I have no idea where he found it or how he even remembered that this was it, but I can't help but smile. I remember how sweet he was to me that night. He sat and let me talk his ear off. He let his friends leave him with me not even knowing my name. He took me out for breakfast food and the least I could do was pay for how sweet he was the entire night. He never tried to push up on me or touch me inappropriately and that is what made him attractive to me. He could've tried to take advantage of the crying girl in the corner, but he didn't. He saw me as a woman and not some quick fling. I can't help but smile at the fact that he remembers that this is what I wore. I put the dress on and to my surprise it still fits. Doing a little spin in front of the mirror I still look as good as I did almost two years ago. I go back into the bathroom and try to decide what hair style to showcase today. Seeing my scarf lying on top of my hair products bin I make the quick decision to wrap my hair into an updo today. As I'm struggling to stuff this 4c hair up neatly, I'm mentally placing shoes with this outfit.

My hair finally cooperates so I move back to the closet. Looking at my shoes the only pair that would look halfway decent are my red sandals. My eyes are already rolling but I suck it up and grab the sandals. This is so not something I would put on myself, but it was my bright idea to agree to this so who can I be mad at. I stand in front our full body mirror in the closet and I can already feel myself being sick. If this is what he wants to see me in I can and play along. Now for the fun part.

I'm looking through Donathan's clothes and I have no idea which direction to lean in. I don't want to pick something for him that he would normally wear. All this man has is suits and warmups. I walk over to the section of his clothes he calls his Gift Garage. Yes, he has a part of the closet he dedicates to gifts he never wears. I know it's weird you don't have to convince me, it's him with the problem. I'm pushing past shirt after shirt and I see it. The first article of clothing I ever got him was a faded peach colored t-shirt. I wanted my man to look chic and stylish, but we see what section of the closet I ended up in. I take the shirt and go lay it out on the bed. I go back to see

28

what pants options he has. Now if I was evil, I would take one of the pants from his suits and make him where them today. I giggle to myself and move over to where I know he keeps his more casual pants. I pick the gray ones and move along to pick out his shoes. Going with the more casual vibe for our event filled day, I pick out his all-white sneakers. He's going to think I'm crazy because he never wears them but what better day than your last. I walk back into the bedroom and lay his items on the bed.

Walking into the kitchen I smell wonderful goodness in the air. Seeing him in the kitchen with his apron on is when he's at his sexiest. I walk up behind Donathan and put my arms around him. "It sure does smell great in here love," I say. He's too tall for me to even think about looking over his shoulder so I come around his side to see what he has cooking. He has eggs on the stovetop, grits in a pot, crispy bacon and juicy sausage already done, and is flipping pancakes. I've never seen this chef of man in the kitchen before, but I have no complaints. I ask him what all this is about, and he tells me it goes with my dress.

29

By now I've come around and taken a seat at the island. I look down at my dress and try hard to fake like I don't know the memory he's trying to recreate. "You do know where that dress is from right?" he asks me. Of course, I explain it's the dress I wore on our first date and he smiles. I'm still trying to fake like I don't recognize this meal, so I don't say anything else. Donathan takes a little of everything and puts it on a plate for me. I wait for him to fix his own plate before I dig in.

We eat in silence for a while and then I give in. I don't know if it's the dress or the food, but I don't resist the urge to walk over to Donathan and give him a kiss on the cheek. This man is so amazing. I walk back over to my plate so that I'm able to finish my breakfast. Still looking down at his plate he says, "You're lucky you got it right. You almost lost your plate." I laugh because I know he's not joking with me. We finish our breakfast and I offer to wash dishes.

As I'm washing dishes, I see Donathan across the room looking out the window. I put the plates back up in the cabinet and I walk over to where he is

"What's wrong Don?" I ask him. He doesn't say anything back, he grabs my hand and guides me to stand in front of him.

I see it. He's staring at how beautiful the sky looks. It almost seems to have a sparkle to it today. From behind me, he whispers, "That's the most beautiful sky I've ever seen." I agree with him, but I know that he doesn't just mean the sky looks nice. "This has to mean something for it too look like that right?" he asks me. I have no answer for him, so I do the only thing I know how to do. Turning around, I hug him. I hold him as tight as I can. I don't know if he takes my hug as an answer, but he hugs me back. I tell him thank you for making such a thoughtful breakfast and I can feel him smile against my cheek.

While I have him distracted, I rush him off to go get dressed, so we won't be late for our first adventure. "Vorie, where are we even going?" he asks me as he laughs at my small physique trying to push him along. I have no idea what to pick yet but I mention it's going to be a surprise. He smiles at me and just shakes his head closing the bathroom door.

31

I turn around and make a dash to the list I left in the living room. I sit on the couch and try to decide what's the first thing I want us to tackle. After choosing to start the day off with a bang, I grab my cellphone and make our reservation.

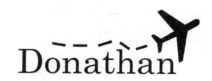

Donathan

We pull up to the address she gives me,
and I see a sign that says Diving Fever. Now I know
this girl isn't wrapped too tight but I'm praying she
hasn't brought me to where the sign implies we are. I
park the car and look in her direction. Vorie's looking
out the window and I know she can feel me staring at
the side of her face. "Sweetheart where are we right
now," I ask her. She slowly starts to turn her head my
way and I can see she's blushing. "We're at a
skydiving place, Donathan. I thought it would be a
fun way to start the day," she tells me. On the inside,
I'm flipping out but on the outside, I don't want to let
her see how startled I am. I try to play it off and say,
"Oh I see."

We get out of the car and find our way to the
main building. Walking inside there's a huge plane, a
wall full of jumpsuit looking things, and a section
with chairs & TVs. I follow Vorie to this window in
the corner. A woman opens the sliding door and asks

if we have an appointment. Vorie shows her some confirmation number on her phone, and we get the green light to pick a jumpsuit. We walk over to the wall of jumpsuits and I'm looking for my size. She has no problem finding hers because she's so small but of course it takes me a while to find an X-Large. After we get suited, we're instructed to take a seat in the chairs in front of the TV.

As we're waiting for others to show up, my hands start to get sweaty. I don't want her to notice that my palms are soaking terribly, so I put them between my legs. She's sitting next to me so calm just taking the place in and I'm losing my mind here. Person after person the seating around us starts to fill up. Our instructor comes out with a huge smile on her face and somehow that makes my nerves worst.

She introduces herself as Farryn and welcomes everyone who will be skydiving today. After hearing her introduction, she tells us that we must sit through an actual training video. After that we will have the opportunity to sign safety waivers. Hopefully, after watching this I'll feel safer. It starts with guys soaring in the sky and I can feel my stomach drop watching them amongst the clouds. The video goes through how we'll be jumping, plane etiquette, and landing form. When the narrator in the video says we'll be up 13,500 ft I can feel my stomach make a descend to the bottom of my shoes. I don't think I'm cut out for this, but I know for a fact the contents of my stomach is not. I'm watching this video and the numbers that I'm hearing aren't adding up to me. We're supposed to be falling 100-120 mph! Who in their right mind would agree to something like that? I take a look around and no one else seemed to be as freaked out as much as I am.

As the video wraps up Farryn comes back out to stand in front of the group. While trying to soak in everything that was said she asks, "Is everyone ready to sign waivers now?" The whole group cheers ready to sign their souls away and I can only sit here and take in what's happening around me. The papers make their way down our row and I notice that they're already filled out, we just have to sign our name. Wanting to be fully informed I start to read my waiver. I'm making it a point to ingest each word when I hear a nasty cough behind me. Intrigued on who could produce such a vile thing I look to the place where the cough could've come from. To my surprise, the whole group is looking at me. Embarrassed I sign the waiver and pass it down. Once Farryn is holding the stack of papers we're instructed to get in a line and take a harness.

I'm behind Vorie and I whisper in her ear that I don't know if I can do this. She turns around and looks at me like I took the last curly fry from the bottom of her bag. "Man up baby," she tells me. I'm not going to lie that one hurt a little bit. She's acting like we're not going to be free-falling toward the earth at lightning speed. Even if today is our last day on earth I want all my hours, I don't want any accidents cutting me short. Before I can respond to her we're at the front of the line. We take the harnesses and step to the side.

Farryn comes in front of us and says she'll be giving us a tutorial on how to put the harnesses on. I try to follow her lead but getting my 6'3 body into some straps showed itself to be difficult. After untangling myself I feel like I'm making some type of progress. Farryn goes around and tightens the straps on everyone's harness. When she gets to me my nerves come back almost instantaneously.

We walk outside and there is a rack of black backpacks. I don't want to seem dumb, but I want to know how a large piece of material that will save my life fit into some college student's backpack. A group almost as big as ours comes to join us and they're already dressed for the plane. They walk past the row of bags, each picking one up on the way toward us. Farryn introduces them as the veteran jumpers and the air in my lungs start to depreciate. I'm about to strap onto one of them and free-fall out of the sky. As a collective we get into a semicircle. The group goes through the motions of how we'll be strapped to the veterans in the sky.

Farryn asks if anyone have any questions. Nobody says a word. I hear, "How many skydiving deaths are there in a year?" I'm looking around to see who would ask a dumb question like that. As I'm looking from face to face, I notice that everyone is staring at me. I know good and well I didn't ask that aloud. Vorie pinches me under my arm, and I bite my tongue trying not to yelp in pain. The instructor smiles and replies that there's a 0.0007% chance of dying from skydiving. Everyone does a sigh of relief like that was a good answer, but my stomach does a backflip.

It's time for us to board the plane and I'm looking for any exit I can take. As if reading my mind, Vorie grabs my hand and ushers me her way. Her soft touch sends chills down my spine. We get in line at the plane and I'm thinking of dropping her hand and making a run for it. I see an older couple at the front of the line that's over twice our age. They seem so calm boarding the plane I'm almost embarrassed at how I'm acting. I attempt to pull myself together and wait our turn.

We're at the front now and I help Vorie climb into the plane. When I get up I see rows and rows of people straddling these carpeted benches. I take the only seat left in the front by the door. Now the little control of my nerves I was holding onto slips away. Vorie hands me a seatbelt that I strap on and pull as tight as I can. From the outside of the plane someone closes the door. Farryn yells from behind us that the plane is about to take off. It'll take twenty minutes for us to get to the right altitude we need to jump. So not only am I the lucky one that gets it sit by the door, I also get to try and not soil my pants for the next twenty minutes. The plane jerks us forward and starts to roll down the runway. We take a bumpy ride down the twist and turns of the airstrip and now it's time for the real take off. We shoot forward and I can feel the plane start to tilt up. I don't even notice that my hand is gripping Vorie's knee.

We're coasting in the air for a short period of time and I'm starting to feel a sense of comfort. I close my eyes and enjoy the motion of the plane. My relaxation is short-lived when I hear a loud swishing sound and feel a sudden aggressive thrust of air. I open my eyes and the door is open. If I wasn't already strapped in with this seatbelt I would've fell out on the floor.

Farryn makes her way to the front and asks who would like to jump first. I get comfortable in my seat because I know I'm not volunteering to go anytime soon. The older couple from earlier raises their hands and the whole plane starts to clap. They make their way down the aisle and come up to the front. Two veteran jumpers get up and begin to strap themselves onto the couple. Farryn gives them one last run through on where to place their legs and arms while in the air. Right before we jump we're instructed to say any last words to the remaining members on the plane. The older gentleman looks me in the eye and says, "Time isn't measured by clocks but by the memories you make with the seconds you have." With that, they jump.

Vorie

We watch person after person jump and my nerves start to go down. Each time Farryn asks someone to volunteer, I go to put my hand up and Donathan smacks it down. It gets to the point where there's only one couple before us. They're about to jump and I keep pushing this boy to get up. Leaning up against the window I can see the sea of people gradually get smaller and smaller. I look over at my boyfriend and I see him grabbing his chest. While the instructor is distracted, I lean forward to check on him. "Don are you sure you're down to do this?" I ask. He shakes his head, yes, but I can tell from his body language that he's not telling the truth. I place my hand on his shoulder to reassure him everything will be okay.

We step up onto the platform to jump and the last two jumpers start to attach to our harnesses. Farryn asks who would like to jump first. I would volunteer to go but I know if I do then he won't do it. I tell Donathan he should go. This man is looking at me like I have betrayed him. He agrees to go but I know he's not happy about it at all. Farryn tells him it's nothing to be scared of. He nods his head like he understands but his body is stuck like a statue. I want to laugh but I don't want to hurt his feelings. I whisper to her is there any other way to get him out of this plane, because he's not going to be able to do that. She walks over to him and says, "If you'd like to sit down on the edge and have Dakota here push you guys off, you could do that." This solution is more up his alley.

He sits on the ground and scoots to the edge of the plane. As soon as he gets to the edge he looks down. I already know we're going to lose him if I don't step in. I waddle up behind him, making my veteran follow behind, and put my hands on his shoulders. I think massaging them will help with the tenseness that I can feel even through these thick suits. He relaxes at my touch but then something happens for the worst. My mind reverts back to this morning and how he pushed me out of bed. I don't want to do it but before I can even stop myself, I push the back of his tandem instructor. I cover my mouth as I see him flailing down toward the earth. I look over at Farryn and she's staring at me. I feel so bad, but he deserved it for what he did to me.

I hear his screams, but I can't look away from her. "Well that's one way to do it," she says to me and that's what breaks my mold. I laugh. I don't mean to because I helped push my boyfriend out of a plane. She tells me we have to jump now so the plane can land. I come up to the edge of the platform and look down. The view is the scariest and most beautiful thing I've ever seen in my life. I lift my hands up, close my eyes, and let my veteran flyer propel us into the sky.

I can feel the breeze take me. I'm floating through the air and I can feel it. My body is twirling in circles and I'm like a majestic bird. I open my eyes and I can see everything. I see the clouds, the sun, and the birds. I'm so close I can touch it all. The ground looks like rectangles and squares. From up here everything looks so minimal. This must be God's view of us since he's so high in the sky. I wonder if we look like microscopic germs to him infecting the earth

45

he built for us to cherish. I hear a beep come from the pack on my back and I realize I'm getting closer to the ground. My veteran pulls our ripcord and the parachute begins to unfold out the backpack. It fills with wind and we're jerked back hard. He offers me the control lines and for a quick second I'm the one that gets to steer us down.

It takes us a while but eventually we slide to a clean landing on the ground. Our parachute starts to come from behind and close in around us. Struggling to find a way out, I see a hand reach inside and grab for my arm. I'm helped up and unwrapped from this huge piece of nylon. Donathan has the biggest smile on his face that I've seen in months. "That was so much fun babe, did you see how everything looked coming down?" he asks me. I smile and happily shake my head yes. He helps me get unstrapped from my tandem instructor and we start our long walk back to where we came from.

The walk there is long but on the way I take this time to look at the nature around us. Sometimes it's so easy to get caught up in our phones or having our heads down that we forget how breath taking this world is.

Getting back to the main building we leave our harnesses in a pile with the others. Following everyone we take our jumpsuits off and put them in a bin labeled used. Retrieving our belongings, we walk hand and hand to the car with him being so joyous. He tells me, "If the rest of the day is anything like now, I'm ready to spend it with you." I grab his face and kiss him because ... I don't need a reason, he's for me. I pull the little crumbled paper out my pocket and we try to decide what we could do next. Donathan comes up with the idea to close his eyes and point to something on the paper. I agree. When he opens his eyes we see his finger landed on paint together. I'm so excited because this is one of the first things I put on our list. I hop in the car eager to go and he shakes his head at me. The car starts and we're off.

Donathan

We pull into this shopping center and I see
this huge sign that says "Paintique". I've only seen
this place on a pass by, but I thought this would be
the perfect place to take her. I park the car and can
see from how she's fidgeting in her seat that Vorie is
excited. I get out and race around to the other side of
the car so that I can open her door. As she's getting
out of the car, I bow and asks for her hand. She
laughs but places her hand in mine. I close the car
door and escort her inside.

Once we're inside a young woman behind the
counter ask if she can help us. I request that we
would like to have a couples painting session right
now. The place is empty, so we have no problem
receiving help. She asks us to look around at the
paintings on the wall and choose a stencil that we
would look like to paint. While Vorie walks away to
have a look at what they have I pay for our session.

I look around and nothing is screaming paint
me. I walk over and ask Vorie if she sees anything she

51

likes. Being the indecisive woman she is of course she isn't ready to decide. I chuckle to myself because I know she won't pick any of them. I step back and let her continue to look. Watching the way she moves I notice the mannerisms she makes when she's struggling to make a decision. I never noticed how she taps her fingers against her right leg when she's looking deeply into something. The little shuffle she does when she can't make up her mind to go left or right. The way she scratches her eyebrow when she's getting frustrated. I realize there is more to this beautiful woman that I still don't know. How many things about her have I brushed over and not noticed? When we first got together I used to pay a lot of attention to the things she would do in an attempt to understand her. Somewhere along the way I got comfortable in winning the girl that I forgot to keep learning my mate. I walk up behind her and give her a hug. "What's that for hun?," she asks me. I just say because I adore you.

As I predicted she didn't like any of the already done paintings. I should've put some money on that bet. I come up with the idea to freestyle our paintings.

I tell her about it and her face lights up. To make things interesting I add that we can't exchange painting until we're finished. The theme we chose to paint was a version of your heart. With these rules in place she agrees, and we walk up to the desk to tell the attendant our decision. She comes from the back and I see her nametag reads Livia. I call her name, get her attention, and she makes her way over to us. I inform her on what we've decided, and she thinks it is very romantic. We wait in the front as she gets the supplies to set up our private station.

When she's done Livia comes to escort us to the back. We follow her past tables and easels deeper into the establishment. We come around the corner and I see one of the most beautiful set ups I've ever seen. Centered in the room are our canvases, easels, and a cart of paint. She also set up some candles and a bottle of wine rested in an ice bucket next to two glasses. A thin layer of rose petals covered the floor and soft romantic music played throughout the room. Vorie gasp when she first walks in. She asks me did I plan all this and of course like a fool I reply yes. I look over at Livia and she winks at me. *Oh she's good.* While

53

Vorie is looking at all the nice decorations I reach in my wallet and slip Livia a fifty dollar bill. She nods and starts to leave the room.

Since nobody's here at the moment she tells us that we can take our time. On her way out she cuts the lights so all we have to use is sunlight. This girl definitely knows how to set a mood. I walk over to Vorie and she is on the verge of tears. "Everything is so pretty babe, you really thought of everything," she tells me. I kiss her forehead and tell her only the best for my queen. I take the bottle of wine and pop it open. As the gentleman I am, I pour her glass first then pour one for myself. "Make a toast Don," she tells me. When she put me on the spot all the words in my head disappear. To buy some time I down my glass and pour another. Holding up my refilled glass I say, "To the greatest day with the greatest woman. On earth and in heaven we are bound." We touch glasses and sip. I ask her if she figured out what she wants to paint yet, and of course her answer is no.

We take seats in front of our opposite facing canvases as she asks me if I've decided what I'm painting, and I declare I'll be painting my heart. From her facial expression I can see that she doesn't get what I'm saying, but I know she will once I'm done.

I get up and walk over to the paint cart that Livia has put in here. I look at the colors and try to decide on how I can pull off what my vision is. I want to do a portrait of her capturing the essence of how radiant she looks today. She looks so beautiful and her wearing this dress is bringing on all types of feeling.

I don't see her skin tone, so I grab all the closest colors I see. Hopefully I can mix something together and get it right. I take all the bottles over to my canvas and try to form a picture of this in my head. I'm squirting colors all over this plate and I start to feel a little in over my head. I'm mixing them and I look up to find her staring out the window. I want to asks her what's wrong, but this is the pose I want her in. I grab a pencil and quickly sketch her looking out this window.

I get my colors together and pick up a brush. I don't know if I'm using the right tools or techniques, but I make a commitment to give it my best shot. I take the paintbrush in my hand, man up, and dip it in

55

a color. I swipe the skin tone I made across her cheek. Now that the first stroke is done, time for me to get in the zone. I keep looking up at her trying to make sure I'm putting the right colors in the correct place. Surprisingly she doesn't appear to notice how hard I'm staring at her. As I'm trying to get the little details right, I notice the small wrinkles she has in her forehead. She has light freckles around her nose that for some reason look so visible today. I look at how the sun hits her light brown eyes and I get butterflies. This woman in front of me is breathtaking and I'm an idiot for not telling her every day. It took some email that I don't even know is real to show me the beauty that I wake up to every morning. I have to get this painting right for her.

I'm working on her eyes and I'm trying to capture the sparkle I see when she looks at me. When I look up I see the look on her face, and I know somethings wrong. "What's wrong Vorie," I ask her. She tells me that she's having trouble thinking of what she wants to paint. I try to say that it doesn't have to be perfect. She nods back at me and I know how to take a hint to shut up. I look back down at my painting and dip into my next color.

Vorie

I'm sitting here looking out this window and nothing is inspiring me. I wanted to come here so bad and now I can't think of anything to paint. I look over at Donathan and he's being freaking Picasso. I'm a little jealous that this is coming so easy to him.

I glance back out the window and I notice the cutest pair of gray birds sitting on a tree branch above our car. They're small and look so in love. The smaller bird has their neck nestled up against the bigger bird's chest. As I'm watching them sit on this tree branch without a care in the world, I wish Donathan and I could take their place. I envy how they can spend the day flying amongst the skies. I wish we could put today behind us and soar endlessly.

For the first time today, I start to think about the time we have left. Chills run over my body. Donathan asks, "What's wrong Vorie?" I tell him I'm having trouble knowing what to paint. I don't want him worrying like I am. We would never enjoy today if that's all we have on our minds. As I glance back at the birds, I see them fly away. They are so gentle with each other and in that moment I know that they are what I want to paint.

I grab a pencil and start to sketch the shape of the birds from memory. I want them to resemble us, so I give them our colored eyes. I walk over to the paint cart to get the colors I need. I realize Donathan has taken all the brown so I walk his way to ask if I can use one. "What are you doing?" he asks to me without even looking up. I stop dead in my tracks. He gets up and brings me a brown. "I said no peaking remember," he reminds me. I want to be annoyed but him taking something I wanted to do seriously is attractive to me. I take the brown he gives me and roll my eyes.

I sit down on my stool and without planning I start to paint. I'm somewhat finding my groove when I start to feel the room get too quiet. I look up and catch Donathan staring at me. He smiles and goes back to painting on his canvas. I wonder what he's over there working on. He's never been the artistic type, but he seems to be very focused over there. I can't have him out doing me, so I kick up my focus and start trying to outdo myself.

After a while of painting I decide to take a bathroom break. I tell Donathan to cover his painting because I know how he feels about his "rules". Once in the bathroom I go to the first stall to avoid an accident. I'm sitting and I hear Livia whispering a few stalls over. Okay yes I started to ease drop but that gives you no room to judge me. We've all don't it before.

I hear her on the phone talking about an email. Now she has my full attention. I can only make out some of the things she's saying. I hear her asks whoever's on the other line if they believe in it. I'm sure they responded yes because she said, "Well I don't, and you shouldn't fall for that scam either."

I wait until she leaves the stall to catch her washing her hands. She comes out of the stall, I wait a couple seconds, then I come out. I can tell she thought she was alone by the look on her face. I walk up to the sink next to her and say hello. "Hi, how are the paintings coming along?" she asks me. I let her know they're coming along great. She turns off the water and I know it has to be here and now. I blurt out "So you got the email too." She takes her hand off the door and turns to me. "What email are you talking about," she asks. I tell her she knows exactly what email I'm talking about. Leaving the door, she starts walking toward me. "How do you know about that email," she yells at me. I explain to her that Donathan and I got it too and that we believe in it. "You've got to be the biggest fools I've ever seen to believe in some scam email from a fake Jesus email address," she says to me. I laugh and pass her as I walk toward the door. I turn back on my way out and say, "See you in heaven or maybe not."

I walk back to our reserved room going straight to the opened bottle. I would've poured a glass but that would've taken a second too long. I take it to the head. "Woah woah woah girl calm down," Donathan says to me. I put the bottle down and laugh as I walk back to my birdies.

I'm painting my birds on my side of the room when I can feel someone staring at the side of my head. I look up and Donathan of course is the culprit. This man has some issues. "May I help you," I ask him. He cheeses and says, "Oh I'm waiting on you to finish so we can show each other." I had no idea that he was finished so now I have to hurry. I make some finishing touches to my background and put my brush down.

Somehow, I trick him into showing me his first. He picks up the painting and flips it so that I can see. I'm speechless. My eyes start to water because this is beyond beautiful. It's me. It's a painting of me staring out the window. I've never seen this man draw as much as a stick figure. I'm so shocked that I don't even realize he's waiting for my response. "Do you like it?" he asks me. I look at him like he's lost his mind. "Like it? Heck no, I love it," I say. He smiles with pride as he sets the painting down to come look at it next to me. I'm so astounded that this looks so much like me. Now I kind of feel like my painting doesn't compare to his. "I told you I was putting my heart on my canvas and that's you sweetie," he says as he hugs me from behind. If I wasn't crying before I definitely am now.

He asks me to show him my painting now. I don't feel as confident anymore, but I grab my canvas and turn it around so that he can see it. I can't read his facial expression and that makes me feel even worse. I explain to him that the two gray kingbirds are what I was staring at out the window and how they represent us to me. They represent how free I wish we could actually be. He's still not saying anything and at this point, I'm a little embarrassed. I'm standing here holding this inferior painting waiting his response. "Vorie this is breathtaking," he said to me. I think he's being nice but by the way he kisses me I know he means it. Sometimes it's not about the quality of the gift but the meaning behind it. As Donathan is picking up both paintings to go put in the car I walk over to the cart of paint. I stick my finger in the red and dot him on the nose. He laughs at me and rubs his face against my cheek. He tells me to go get cleaned up so we can get to his surprise. Now I'm confused because I thought we were following the list today. "Just trust me my love," he says and without hesitation I do.

Donathan

We pull up to Tranquil Gardens. Vorie has been begging me to schedule her an appointment here for months. I took the opportunity to call and handle that while she was in the bathroom earlier. I look over at her and she is smiling from ear to ear and that's exactly what I wanted to see.

I park the car and this girl immediately jumps out. I can't help but to laugh at her silliness. I get out the car and meet her inside. She's already at the counter giving them my name. I walk up and the woman already has her hand out ready for my card. I reach for my wallet and hand it to her. She hands us a service menu and tells us to pick which massage we would like. Vorie goes to ask my opinion, and I let her know this is her gift she has to pick. We're glancing over each package to see what they offer, and I never thought there were so many types of massages. I mean the Swedish, the deep tissue, the reflexology (I

don't even know what that means), and the list goes
on and on. I may not know what these things consist
of, but I know what acupressure means and I express
to her I want no parts of it. After being rudely called
lame she chooses the full body massage with a few
added on surprises. That surprise made me feel iffy,
but I decided to trust her praying this wouldn't bite
me in the end. After we tell the associate our decision,
she smiles and says perfect. She swipes my card and
gives it back on top of some folded robes.

All I know of massage places is what I see in
the movies. I thought this would be a long shot but
even so I asked, "Do you guys have a mud bath here?"
She shakes her head yes and now I'm the excited one.
I put on my puppy dog eyes and I look over at Vorie. I
don't think the face is very good, but she still tells me
yes. I give the woman my card again and pay for a
thirty-minute mud bath. Giving me my card back this
time she hands over two locker keys. "If you walk
down that hallway right there you will find the locker
rooms and complimentary swimsuit bins," she says.
Grabbing Vorie's hand we start our walk.

We make it to the bins and I'm a little surprised that she was telling the truth. Checking tags I eventually find some trunks in my size. While Vorie looks through the bikinis I take the opportunity to go into the locker room and get changed.

This place is amazing. They have wall mounted Tv's in here, huge recliner chairs, and everything looks so clean. I walk past a couple of rows of lockers until I find the number that matches the key in my hand. I open it and there's already a gift inside. It sucks I'll only be able to come here once because I think I'm in love. I open the package and there's a pair of ear plugs. I can't tell you I know what they're for, but it doesn't matter cause it's free. I slam the locker shut and rush to go get changed.

Coming out of the bathroom, I sprint to put my clothes up. I grab my key & ear plugs ready to go. There is a pyramid of towels on the way out and I take one. Once I'm in the hallway I see Vorie's not out yet. Taking a seat to wait for her I start to look at the décor of the place. They definitely have mastered the art of investing in themselves.

Another worker comes from the direction of the front desk and walks my way. When he reaches me, he asks if I would like to be escorted to the mud pool. Before I could tell him I'm was waiting on someone Vorie she comes out. I'm not going to lie to you my eyes immediately go to her in the bathing suit. This simple black bikini looks so amazing on her cream colored skin. "Are you ready to go?" she asks me and that's when I realize I'm staring at her. I grab her hand and I let the attendant lead the way. We walk down the halls of this establishment and we come up to this weird looking door. We're instructed to leave our towels outside on a rack due to the mud being everywhere inside.

As he leaves, I open the door for Vorie to enter. Walking in after her I see that he wasn't kidding about the mud being everywhere. We're in this room that appears to be made out of mud with a huge pool of it in the floor. I get closer to the mud and I realize that it's bubbling. Seeing this mud bath in person and thinking of how long I've wanted to try this, I hop in with no hesitation. The initial feeling of the warm mud consuming me felt glorious. I turn around and take Vorie's hand trying to guide her into the bath. Looking at her face I know she's loving this as much as I am. We sit on the bench inside and now it's up to our chest. "How you liking it babe?" I ask Vorie. She tells me this feels great. I take my ear plugs and put them in. Leaning back, I try to relax.

Soaking this in, I can feel Vorie get comfortable against me. The warm feeling starts to take over and my mind starts to wonder. It flows to what tomorrow morning will bring. I don't want to think about these things, but it's impossible to act like I didn't read that email this morning. I wonder things like will it hurt, will it be quick, and will me and Vorie be together. What if I get to heaven and I have no memory of her? Or what if I remember her but I can't find her? The uncertainty of what to expect is horrifying. Why didn't we know that we were so in the wrong? I knew the world we lived in was crazy, but I never thought it was ever a possibility that God would get so upset he'd end it. I guess I can't even be mad at him. If people treated something I made like we do this earth, I'd take my gift back too. I hadn't noticed that I pulled Vorie closer to me. I may not know what's to come but I'll hold her close while I still can.

We sit in this pool for twenty minutes with me holding her. No words have to be spoken. Our company was enough. The attendant comes back and taps me on the shoulder to tell us that our time is up. I help Vorie walk over to the stairs so she can get out the pool first. We're out and instantly the mud starts to dry. He tells us the quicker we get to the showers the easier it'll be to get it off. We grab our towels from the rack outside the room. He guides us back to the locker rooms. Before leaving us to freshen up, he tells us to put on the robes and someone will be back to escort us to our massage room. I ask Vorie one more time if she's enjoying herself before we split up. She comes over, kisses me, and walks into the woman's locker room. I'm guessing that was a yes. Turning around I head to handle my own dirt.

Vorie

I never knew mud was so hard to get off.
I'm in here showering & scrubbing places I never
thought would have mud in them. The mud bath was
so soothing I adored it. After getting what would
agree to come off down the drain, I cut the water off.
Taking a new towel from the freshly washed stack, I
wrap it around and walk to my locker. Tying my hair
up in a tight bun, I throw the robe on and walk
toward the exit. I've been looking forward to the
massage for the past thirty minutes. I walk out the
locker room and for a change I'm the first one ready.
The worker is in the hall already and I decide to stop
being rude and asks him his name. He tells me it's
Saxton and I respond, "That's a beautiful name."
Before we can say anything else Donathan comes out
the locker room. Saxton leads us into the room we're
getting our massages in.

When we walk in the room and there are two
workers in uniforms in the corner. The masseuse and
masseur introduce themselves to us as Avah and

Jase. We are instructed to take our robes off and use the towels on the beds to cover our bottoms. Donathan looks at Jase, looks at me, then raises his eyebrows. All I can do is laugh at this man. He takes his towel and shields me as I take my robe off to lay down. I take the towel from under me and cover my butt with it. With a quick glance to see if someone was watching Donathan walks over to his bed. While they're still distracted, Donathan throws his robe on the floor as he jumps onto the massage table in a hurry. I'm going to blow a vessel trying to keep myself from screaming out in laughter. Avah walks over to me and ask am I ready to start my massage. Eagerly I say yes and to start with the add ons that I selected. I didn't tell Donathan that I added on some hot stones for us. Avah and Jase come back with a steaming bowl for each of us. Donathan with bulged eyes asks, "What is that for?" I tell him to trust me like he told me to trust him. He narrows his eyes at me, but he doesn't say anything else. Avah goes over to the switch on the wall and turns down the lights. Jase walks over to the stereo and puts on some slow instrumental music.

My body is anticipating this treatment. Both of them coat our backs in some type of oil that smells fantastic. Avah puts the rocks in a line on my back. I flinch because they're so hot. As they sit there, I can feel then loosen my muscles in my back. I look up at Donathan and he looks like he wants to scream at me. I giggle to myself because I know he won't cause a scene in front of them.

She starts to move the rocks across my back, and this feels like nothing I've ever felt in my life. I could go to sleep laying right here on this table with her making these small circles with the rocks. I check on Donathan again and now he seems to be enjoying this a lot more than before.

We lay like this for a few minutes until the rocks cool off. Taking the rocks off I know it's time for my next surprise. Now I know that Donathan said that he didn't want to do acupressure, but that's because he's being scary. I see them bring the needles over but Donathan is still laying with his face down. I pray he doesn't go ballistic. I barely feel her stick me with the first one. It doesn't feel as bad as people make it seem.

I can feel them all in my shoulder area, but I don't know where else she's stuck them.

I hear Donathan ask what is taking so long and I know that means he doesn't feel what's going on. All I say is that we're waiting for the oils to heat up. Avah whispers in my ear that we have to lay like this for 5 minutes. I whisper back okay and tell Donathan, "Only a couple more minutes."

After the 5 minutes have come and gone, they both come over to remove the pins. Avah takes all mine out and I can feel a weight lift off my back. I glance up and Jase is taking the last of Donathan's out and he still hasn't said anything. Once he's a safe distance from him I tell Donathan to look up. He obeys and asks, "Are the oils almost ready?" I can't help but pity my poor boyfriend. I confess that we had a session of acupressure. He eyes expand to the biggest I've ever seen them in my life. It almost looks as if they are about to pop out. He tells me I better be lying, and I try to sweeten the blow by saying he didn't even feel it. Jase asks him, "Sir how does your back feel now?" He stretches out a little and with a skeptical look on his face he says it feels better. I take this as my opportunity to say, "See that's because of the acupressure." He eyeballs me and says he never should've trusted me. I blow him a kiss and smile. Now it's time for what I've been waiting on. The two of them come back over with the real oils this time. Donathan makes Jase promise that he won't stick him with anything before he puts his head back down. I can't help but to laugh.

When Avah starts my massage, I swear I can feel an angel's wings go over my back. Her hands are so strong they are just taking everything that's been on my mind away. The soothing feeling starts to put me in a trance. Donathan asks me how I'm enjoying myself and I can't help but moan out a thank you for bringing me here. Of course, he laughs at me and we lay here finishing these blessings of massages.

Once our massages are done, they tell us that we can go back into the locker room and get dressed. They walk out so we can put our robes back on. I get up and my body feels like a noodle. I get to my robe and put it on. Donathan waits for me at the door so we can walk out together. He grabs my hand which he knows I love, and we make our way back down the hall. Reaching the locker rooms we split to get dressed.

As I'm standing in front of the locker to get my clothes, I realize that I am starving. I'll bring it up when we get in the car and I hope he's starving too. I put my clothes back on and grab my purse. Bringing my dirty towels to the door, I drop them in the dirty bin. When I come out the locker room Donathan isn't waiting for me, so I assume he's still in the locker room. I sit in the big chair across the hall and I wait for him to come out.

Avah comes down the hall toward the dressing room. I reach into my purse and pull out a twenty-dollar bill for her. When she reaches me, I grab her hand and give it to her. She asks me what it's for and I reply for giving me the best massage I've ever had. I'm thanked and then she's on her way. Donathan comes out with his things and the first thing I say is, "I'm starving." He laughs at me and says he was going to suggest we get something to eat. As we're walking to the car, I ask him what he has in mind and of course he doesn't know. Men try to make it seem like women never know what they want but it's definitely the other way around. I suggest we go to his favorite burrito place because I know he loves Hispanic food and his face lights up.

Now he's rushing me in the car and running around to the other side. I complain that I don't want to eat it inside because we're kind of on a time crunch and I don't want to waste a minute. He agrees and suggest that we get our food togo and eat it at a nearby park. I pull our list out of my purse and a picnic in the park is on there, so I decide why not.

Donathan

We pull up to Midnight Foodies and I'm
already halfway out the car before I even put the gear
shift into park. I waste no time getting in line and
looking at the menu. I hear Vorie get out the car and
walk up behind me. I don't have to turn around to
know that she's laughing at me. Normally I'm a
gentleman but this place does something to me. Since
my first time here I've been hooked on them and only
them. I decide that if this is going to be my last day on
earth I'm going out with a bang. I decide to get one of
everything to try. I ask Vorie if she knows what she
wants, and she replies a quesadilla meal. Wherever
we go rather it's a restaurant or food truck if
quesadillas are an option that's what she's getting.

It's my turn to order so I tell the server I'd like
one of everything. He stares at me for a little bit then
repeats, "One of everything?" I repeat my order to him
a second time. He ask me, "You know what will be
very expensive right?" I nod my head yes and add an
extra quesadilla meal. He tells me that it will take a

while for the food to cook, so we can go sit in our car and he'll get our attention when it's done.

As we walk back to the car Vorie's on her phone. I ask her what she's looking at and she tells me nothing. I don't want to press the subject (especially not today), so I open her door letting her in. Walking around I get in. I turn up the radio and the one thing I didn't expect to be happening happens.

"Hello listeners! Thank you for tuning into 80.2 HotterThanHot this lovely afternoon. Now the topic on the chopping block today is the talk about this crazy email that I got in my inbox this morning. Apparently, I'm not the only one that's gotten it. For those of you who haven't checked your emails yet, there is an email sent out from a username claiming to be Jesus. It's saying that God is coming to shut the world down tomorrow. I don't know if I believe it or not but tell me your thoughts. Call (829)637-9200."

I'm so taken aback by this radio broadcast. We've been to so many places already today and nobody has brought it up yet. When I look over at

Vorie she's staring at me. I can tell from the look in her eyes that she's feeling uneasy. I grab her hand to comfort her and she tells me to turn the radio up. I ask her if she's sure and she shakes her head yes. I turn up the radio and we listen some more.

We sit and listen to person after person call the station and give their opinions on what is happening. Some believe, some care to argue that it's the government, and some don't even feel the need to open the email. It's crazy to think that in eighteen hours we'll have our final answer.

I see something moving in my line of vision and I look up to the server waving at me. I tell Vorie I'll be back and get out to go pay for the food. Carrying about three bags of some pretty heavy food I wobble back to the car. I put the food in the back and walk around to get into the driver's seat. This girl is still listening to the radio. I turn it down and she looks at me as if to ask what I'm doing. I tell her, "If we keep listening to this it'll only continue to feed our fears. If you really want to get something off your chest, we can do that at the park but listening to that will only make our day worse." She agrees with me and I drive off into the direction of the park.

When we pull up, and it's awfully empty. I pop the trunk so that Vorie can get the blankets out the back, and I go for the food. I wait until she's ready and we start our walk to find the perfect spot to sit.

I find this spot in sort of the middle of an open field and it's a beautiful place to sit. Getting Vorie's attention so we can set up, I put the food down and help her layout the blankets. I'm watching her put all the food out and I get an idea. I wait until she's done, and I take her plate away. "Hey! I'm hungry! What are you doing?" she questions me. I laugh and tell her if I'm going to try everything from my favorite place food truck in the world that she's going to do it with me. She looks at me like I'm a lunatic at first, but I negotiate saving her meal for if she doesn't like anything we try. After I tell her that I see she starts to calm down a little. I put her plate behind me and ask her where she would like to start. She finally gives in to me and picks the spinach & cheese enchiladas. I know it'll be something she likes; I just can't wait to see her fake like it's not. I give her a fork

and I let her break off a piece first. She waits for me
to get mine so we can try them together. I break mine
off and at the same time we put both pieces into our
mouths. I see her face light up, but she quickly
controls it. I give her a minute to savor the taste
before I lay into her. "So, how'd you like it," I ask. She
tries to look at me with a straight face but I'm already
grinning.

Laughing she replies it was okay. I know she's
trying to play it modest because I've been asking her
to try something new from this place for what feels
like forever now. Trying to get her to expand her food
palette is like trying to fit a size six stiletto pump onto
a raging bull. I asks her if she would like another
taste before I practically kill this plate and to my
surprise she says yes. I pull a plate out the bag and
take a whole piece out to give to her. I know I'll never
get a you're right but it's enough that she asked for
more.

After we finish the enchiladas, I'm ready to move onto
the fajitas. I don't want to scare her tongue too much
but while I've got her on the line I have to reel her
fully in. I take out a tortilla, put all the fixings in it,

and roll it up. She's already looking skeptical about it, but I give it to her. She tries to wait for me to make my own, but I want to give her my full attention on this one. She takes a bite and a mmmmm slips out. It takes both she and I by surprise. At least I don't have to ask her if she liked it.

I make my own and down it quick. When I look up at her she's staring at me. I take the liberty of making her another one because I already know that's what she wants. I hand it over and she gets all giddy like a schoolgirl. Before I can ask her what she would like to try next she's already going through the togo containers. I sit back and let her do her thing. She hands me the bag to take the food out and it's exactly what I wanted. I love how in sync we are.

Vrie

I dislike him. I refuse to tell him that he's
right. I've never tried anything new from Midnight
Foodies. Once I get into the habit of something I hate
to stray away, but this food is so good. He'll never get
the satisfaction of hearing it from my mouth though.
He hands me a plate with two tacos on it and tells me
that they're fish tacos. I'm iffy on fish being in tacos
but I commit to giving it a try. He's sitting here staring
at me, so I know that means he's waiting to see my
reaction. I pick up one taco and I take a bite. To my
surprise, like everything else, these tacos are
delicious. I've been trying my hardest to hide my
facial expressions, but I know I'm not doing a good
job. I can't tell him that he's completely right, but I
give in a little and tell him, "These are really good."
He smiles his proud satisfactory grin and fixes two
tacos for himself.

I'm starting to get full, but we have so much
more food to try. Next I ask if we can taste the
quesadillas. He agrees to try them. Reaching behind

his back he gives me my plate that he's been hiding from me. I wait as he looks through the bags to find the right container for himself. He opens it and before he picks up a piece he looks at me. "Oh, I'm waiting on your reaction." I say. I watch as he tries it and I can see his face turn. "This is what you been getting all this time?" he asks. Instantly I'm offended. I jump onto him with the food in his hands. He falls back and the piece of quesadilla goes flying. My hands are around his neck and he's choking from laughter. "Tap out," I yell at him. He taps on the ground and tries to catch his breath. I get off him and let him up. He's still trying to catch his breath as I move back to where I was sitting before. "I was joking my love. It's good," he tells me. I'm still eye balling him as he collects himself. He catches his breath and takes another piece of quesadilla. I continue to finish my meal, but we eat in silence.

My stomach is on the verge of combusting. I can't try anything else and I don't think he can either. I lay back on the blanket and look up at the sky. It's such a vibrant blue. Donathan moves the food containers out the way and lays next to me. He grabs my hand and we rest for a second. I can't remember a time that I've ever done this before in my life. When you take the time out to just shut up and listen you can hear the world scream around you. I can hear the trees breathe as the wind flows through them. I can make out the birds in the distance having a full conversation with each other. I hear the sounds of little squirrels moving through the grass. I wonder how bad we messed up the world. I mean you hear people advocate for global warming and how that's hurting us. Hundreds talk about the waste problems we have and how there's more plastic in the ocean than on land. Recently I heard the number of people dying from not having access to clean water is the highest it's ever been. We hear about the problems of this world and the large number of the people it's affecting, and we ignore it. Instead of helping each other to fix the problem we overlook our neighbor until it's happening to us.

The more I think about it the more it upsets me. I'm scared about what could happen tomorrow morning. I want to be upset with God for what he's doing to us, but I know we did this to ourselves. He gave us this world to cherish and we haven't done that. Yes I'm sad but I can't say I don't understand why.

I squeeze Donathan's hand tighter because that's been making me feel better all day. He brushes his thumb across the top of my knuckles and that's all the reassurance I need. "The foods getting cold." I tell Donathan. He tells me to let it and that he'd rather lay with me. I sit up and ask him if he'd like to go for a walk. He replies yes and we start to pack up our things.

I wait for him on the sidewalk as he puts the blankets back in the trunk. He comes back to me and ask why I didn't come put the food in the car. I express we might find somebody to bless along the way. He smiles at me and kisses my hand.

We start our walk around the pond. There are ducklings swimming all throughout the water. I stop and reach into the bag of food to pull out a tortilla. I don't know if this is something ducks can eat but these babies sure look ready to tear it up. Some larger ducks start to make their way toward us, and I know that means it's time to go. We walk around the pond and take a dirt path deeper into the park.

As we walk through the trees it feels like we're entering another world. The deeper we go the more the world we perceive as normal starts to disappear. The nature was pretty before but now we're in a spot where it's beyond simple words. The flowers are so vibrant, types I've never even seen before. I take out my phone and I start to take pictures of the beauty around us. As I'm framing a photo of these breathtaking fire wheel's I've found I see a little tent off into the distance. I bring it to Donathan's attention, and he immediately wants to go the other way. Me being the nosy person I am I walk toward it. He starts to aggressively whisper my name, but I assume he starts to follow me because he soon stops.

When I arrive at the tent I can tell it belongs to someone homeless. It's ripped in some places, dirty in others, and if I must say it had a God-awful smell. I poke my finger through a hole closer to the top and say, "Umm hello?" I mean it wasn't a door so it's not like I could've knocked or rang the doorbell. The tent starts to unzip and for a second I'm thinking what am I doing. Donathan reaches me and takes a stance partially in front of me. A little old man pulls back the fabric and now I feel terrible. "May I help you?" he asks me. I asked him if this is where he lived, and he told me yes. That broke my heart. I take the bags of food that are in my hands and I give them all to him. With a shocked look on his face he takes them. I tell him it's for him and there is enough to save for later. He tells me thank you and shakes my hand. Nodding at Donathan he zips up his tent.

As we're walking out of this secluded area Donathan asked me why I did that. Honestly I had no answer for him. I guess I was blessed to be a blessing to someone else. I say, "We were going to throw it away anyway." We make our way back around the park and end up in front of our car. Donathan grabs my hand and turns me around. "What are you planning on doing next little lady?" he asks me. Up until now I hadn't thought about it. I instruct him to wait right here and I jog over to the back of our car. I take out our list and quickly look over the things that I know he wants to do. I find one and go to google. It doesn't take me long to find a place. I hurry and call to make sure that they're open today. Just my luck they are so I make us a reservation. I walk back over to Donathan and tell him that we have to get going if he wants to make it to his surprise. He smirks at me and walks over to the passenger door. Opening the door for me he turns around when he notices I don't immediately get in. "Oh did I forget to say that I was driving," I say with my hand outstretched for the keys. He shakes his head at me reaching into his pocket pulling them out. He knows better than to pick a fight with me.

Donathan

I'm sitting in the passenger seat with this blind fold on and I haven't the slightest idea of where we're going. She told me it was somewhere I've been wanting to go for a while now and that could be anywhere. The car comes to a stop, so I assume that we're here. "Can I take this thing off now," I ask her and of course she says not yet. I'm sitting waiting for something to happen and I hear her snickering, so I know she's playing with me. I yank the blindfold off and all I see is a sign that says Riding Ridge Stables. Now I want to be excited but I'm not sure we are where I think so I try and play it cool. She sees my reaction and I can tell it's not the one she wanted. "You said you wanted to ride horses right," she asks me. And that's when my face lights up.

I'm bouncing in my seat with excitement like a kid in a candy store. Since my young days I've always wanted to ride a horse like the cowboys did in the movies I used to watch with my granddad. I'm surprised she actually listens to my rambles from when I was a kid. I rush her out the car so we can get inside.

We come up on this small building next to this enormous barn. I open the door for Vorie, and we walk inside. She goes up to the counter and gives them her last name. This must be what she was doing when she went hiding behind the car. The woman behind the counter tells us that we have to go into the barn and pick a horse before we can do anything else.

We walk out the office area and find the entrance to the barn. We go inside and it's an endless row of horses. Now I have never in my life seen a real horse, so I was kind of surprised at their actual size. We walk down the rows and I'm looking at each horse's information card hanging from the outside of their stable. It has their names, how old they are, and what they weigh. I am determined to find the perfect horse for my first and last ride.

I get toward the end of the row and I'm not finding what I'm looking for. In the last stable in the back leaning on a pile of hay I see him. He is what I've been looking for all along. I read his card and it says his name is Nicky. I knew from looking at him that he was the horse for me. A girl comes around the corner and says, "Nicky doesn't do too well with men." I'm assuming she works here because she has on jeans, a flannel shirt, and riding boots. Vorie asks her what her name is, and she replies Ivy. I say, "No offense Ivy but I've been waiting all my life to ride a horse and it has to be a black one." She tells me that I'm doing this at my own risk, and I'm fine with that. I've dreamed of this moment plenty of times through the years and it's always been me riding a black horse. I have to fulfill the prophecy exactly how it was written.

Vorie walks back down the aisle and finally decides on a female horse named Juniber. She was a pretty brown and had white spots all over. Ivy shows us how to unlatch the gate. She tells us that she is only here to be a guide and that we'll actually be the ones interacting with the horses today. This keeps getting better and better.

Vorie walks in first and comes out with Juniber walking on a rope attached to her halter. I go into my stable and Nicky is already making noises at me. Now I'm kind of nervous because I want him to like me, but

I read somewhere that animals can sense fear. I walk over to him and reach for his rope. He lets me take it without snapping at me, so I assume we don't have any bad blood at the moment. I walk him out the stable and Ivy says she's surprised Nicky let me get this close. I'm advised not to get too comfortable because he's known to be full of surprises.

Ivy walks us over to a prep area for the horses. We have to establish a relationship with them before we start riding. She gives us carrots to feed them by hand. When I give Nicky my carrot he sort of snatches it out my hand. I look around to see if anyone else saw that and of course these two seem preoccupied. Ivy tells us that she has to go get her horse to show us how to groom them and saddle up.

When she walks away, I walk over to Vorie and tell her that the horse snatched the carrot from me. She says I'm overreacting and that he must've been hungry. I agree she must be right but I'm still eye balling this horse.

When Ivy comes back she's accompanied by an all-white horse. Now this one is a beauty but doesn't even compare to Nicky. We take our horses and follow her to the grooming station. She tells us that grooming makes the horses calm before the ride. We each take a brush and start with their mane. I'm watching my hands, so they don't get too close to Nicky's mouth, but he looks calmer at the moment. I comb his hair out and then she says it's okay to move to the body. I start brushing and dusting his body off and he doesn't move a muscle. I'm starting to feel more comfortable around him and I think he's starting to like me. I move behind him and Ivy tells me to be very careful not to get kicked. Trying to still be brave I grab its tail. I'm brushing as softly as I can but I pray this horse doesn't kick me on purpose.

I'm almost done brushing his tail so we can move onto the next thing when this over 840-pound animal farts on my hand. The smell hits me like a strong right hook. It was as if a garbage truck was somehow put into a microwave, warmed up, then left out to cool off. My stomach immediately went into knots as soon as he did it. Ivy and Vorie thought it was so funny. I'm on the verge of throwing my entire lunch up and these two are having the time of their lives. I say aloud, "I knew this horse had it out for me."

Vorie tells me to stop being so dramatic and that he probably had gas at the time. As a black man I know when I'm being targeted. I refuse to brush him any longer. I stand there and watch as these two finish brushing their horses. We put the brushes down and Ivy tells us it's time to grab the saddles. We tie the horses up to a post and walk into the stable to get them. Ivy explains that the saddles size is based on the back of the horse. She gives us the correct saddle we need, and boy let me say that these were not light in the slightest.

Dragging them to where the horses are, she gives us a quick lesson on saddling up. I didn't want Vorie lifting that heavy thing, so I pick her saddle up and put it on for her. She does her straps and I move on to do my horse.

Now I'm standing next to him and can feel him staring at me. I'm sensing from his vibe that he has some animosity. I lean closer to him and say, "Please don't ruin this dream for me." For the first time today, he snorts at me. I don't speak horse but I'm assuming that was an okay. I throw the saddle over his back and I fasten my straps under his belly. That went a lot easier than expected so I hope I've proven myself to him. Now that our horses are ready to ride we untie them and walk over to the open pasture.

Vorie

Ivy gives us a demonstration on how to get on our horses. I try and on my first attempt I get on with no problem. Donathan on the other hand, not so much. He puts his foot into the stirrup on the saddle and attempts to throw his leg over. Each time he builds the momentum to get it up Nicky moves. Ivy and I begin to laugh. I don't know if his horse is doing this on purpose, but he is quite the character if he is. "This isn't going to work," he says. I can tell he's starting to feel defeated, so I step in and try to encourage him. "Come on babe, try one more time," I say. He takes a deep breath and kicks his leg over one more time.

As soon as his leg touches down on the other side his horse is off. My mouth drops and my body is stuck. He's holding the horse around the neck and bouncing so high. I hear him screaming but my body won't spring into action. I've never rode a horse before, but I've seen it in the movies. I grab the reins in front of me and I tap the horse with my heels.

Juniber starts to trot and I'm trying my best to follow Donathan. He's getting further and further away from us and I can't see where Nicky is taking him. Ivy says from behind me, "Lean forward and slightly lift up to ask her to go faster." I do what she says, and my horse starts to pick up speed almost immediately.

We're going as fast as we can, and it seems like we aren't getting any closer to Donathan and Nicky. He's taking him all the way to the fencing of the pasture. Deciding not to give up, we keep chasing in hopes that he'll tire out but from the looks of things he is still going strong. I yell behind me, "What are the chances of Nicky jumping that fence?" She says back to me that if he has enough speed (which he does) he could easily clear it. Now, this makes me even more nervous because that horse looks like he's still speeding up. I'm trying to see where he could be going but there's no way to cut him off from back here. Nicky does what looks to be a sharp turn to the right and Donathan goes flying. My heart drops seeing my boyfriend flailing like a rag doll across the sky. I gasp out loud and grip my reins even harder. As we get closer Ivy instructs me on how to slow Juniber down. I bring her to a complete stop, and I hop right off. Running over to Donathan I see he's face down on his stomach. I fall to my knees at his side and I try to roll him onto his back. Flipping him, I put my ear to his chest to make sure that he's still breathing. In my head, I say, "God, please don't take him before our last hours are up." He takes a huge gasp for air. I pick his head up and put it on my lap so he can breathe easier. Donathan struggles to catch his breath and as he does he begins to laugh. Once I see that he is ok I admit I start to laugh a little too. "Are you okay sweetie?" I ask him. He tells him that his chest hurts a little bit but for the most part he feels fine. Ivy comes up to check on him and lets us know that she has to go catch Nicky. I can tell from the look on her face that she wanted to say I told you so, but she was being nice. I let her know it's fine and we can just ride Juniber back. Donathan looks at me like I'm crazy but doesn't say anything. Ivy rides off and when she's far enough away Donathan says, "I'm not getting on another damn horse." I want to laugh and call him a baby, but I know he has a valid reason for being scared. I say, "But Don, Ivy told you that he was difficult to begin with, Juniber isn't like that. I rode her the entire ride up here, and I was fine." He eyeballs Juniber and says he doesn't know about it. I remind him that we are very far away from the stables, and he'll be left to walk if he doesn't come on. He narrows his eyes at me, I'm guessing to see if I'm bluffing or not, and eventually he agrees to come with me.

I hold Juniber steady so that he can get on. I could feel his body shaking through her, so I know he was beyond nervous. I get on in front of him and tell him to grab my waist. Taking the reins in my hands, I tap her underneath her belly again. She takes off slow and I plan to keep it that way so Donathan doesn't lose his mind behind me. We start to make our way back to the stables.

On our stroll, we finally had a chance to look at the scenery we zoomed passed on the way coming. This pasture happens to be very nice. "It's so pretty out here Vorie." he tells me. I swear sometimes this boy can read my mind. Taking in everything around us I start to realize how far Nicky really brought him. We have a longer trip then I thought to the stables.

107

I start to see the barn off in the distance. Ivy is standing outside, and she looks like she's cleaning Nicky. We finally make it back and I walk Juniber up right next to him. We slide off and Ivy asks how was the ride back. I answer her saying it was truly blissful. She tells me that if we're done riding for the day we can walk Juniber back to her stable. I turn to Donathan and ask if he wanted to go riding again. If I could only come up with words to describe how this man looked at me. The closest I could get with common English is furious. Nicky neighed as Ivy was petting him and I guess that meant he felt the same way. I laugh at these two and tell him to follow me. I take Juniber's rope and walk her back to her assigned stable. Before I close the door to it I hug her, in case I never see a horse again. I lock her stable door and grab Donathan's hand. We make our way back into the small office building.

When we walk in the woman behind the counter says it looks like we had fun. I know she's alluding to how dirty Donathan is and I almost bite my tongue off trying to keep from laughing. He just nods her way and we continue to walk back to the bathroom. I go in and carefully wash my hands and try to get the little dirt that's on the bottom of my dress off.

I come out of the restroom and Donathan's still not out yet. I take this opportunity to walk around the store and browse their souvenirs. They have elegant horse art, cute little novelty stuff, and so much more. As I'm looking I feel a tap on my shoulder. I turn around and its Donathan. "What?" I ask him. He tells me that the dirt isn't coming out his pants and that he needs to buy a new pair. I look down and I hate to say it but he's right the pants are goners. We walk over to the clothing section and find the only bottoms available in his size. Sweatpants that read Riding Ridge going down the leg. He's crushed I know he is. Before he can even protest I give him the pair of pants. "We have more things to do today love. Our hour is almost up, and you promised we would stick to the schedule," I say. Even though he doesn't want to he takes the pants and goes to the bathroom to change. I take the tag to the register and I let her know that he's making a quick change. As I'm paying I can feel him come up behind me. I don't even turn around because I know I'm going to laugh in his face if I see his outfit right now. I grab the receipt and we start to head to the car. Donathan puts his arm around me and thanks me for booking this for us but horse riding is not for him. I laugh and tell him where we go next will be a little more his speed. He asks me where exactly might that be and I haven't even looked at the list yet. I wait until we're seated in the car before I pull it out. Next up is kiss on top of a Ferris wheel. "Where the heck are we going to find a Ferris wheel," I ask him. He reminds me of the carnival flyer that we saw earlier at the park. I ask him how do we know for sure they have a Ferris wheel. "There's only one way to find out," he says as he puts the car in drive.

Donathan

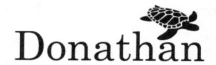

I'm stopped at the traffic light and I can see the Ferris wheel from here. "Look baby I see it," I say. She seems pretty excited to say she's not too fond of heights. I pull into the parking lot and try to find a spot a little closer to the entrance. We park and I walk over to Vorie's door to open it. I take her hand and we make our way to the entrance.

We aren't even at the gate before we hear a worker screaming that you have to pay to get in. I reach for my wallet and already have the money in hand. We get in line and I ask her if she would like to do more than the Ferris wheel. She tells me she won't know until she gets inside. This woman couldn't make up her mind if the fate of the world depended on it. I mean if it did a couple of hours wouldn't matter right?

We get to the front and I give the attendant the money for our tickets. We walk in and as soon as we pass the threshold this woman says she wants a funnel cake. Now neither of us has ever been to this carnival before so we set out on an adventure to find the food trucks.

With no sense of direction, we start walking down rows of games and rides before we finally spot a truck. I walk towards the sitting area to find us a spot while she decides on what flavor she wants. I reach into my pocket and slide her the money.

Finding us a spot right across from the food truck, I take a seat and put my feet up saving her a spot. For the first time today, I take out my phone. Surprisingly, I have no notifications and that hasn't happened since I took the phone out the box. I glance at social media and my threads are looking somewhat normal now. I can't decipher if that's a good or bad thing.

I look up and Vorie's walking toward me. I put my phone down and sit up straight. "Somebody called," she asks. I reply no and that I was glancing on social media. She sort of eyeballs me but doesn't say anything else. "What is this monstrosity of a funnel cake that you've brought V," I ask her. She tells me she got a fruity pebbles funnel cake with extra vanilla icing and whipped cream. I can't lie this thing looked magnificent. I take the plate from her so she can sit down. She pulls out two forks and I get so jumpy. I can feel the sugar coursing through my veins before I even take the first bite. Setting the plate down, I take my fork from her. I let her taste it first because I know if it's good I'm go kill it. She makes this face like it's the best thing she's ever had, and I can't hold myself to being a gentleman any longer. I taste my first fork full. My head explodes, my heart pops and my body collapses. This is the closest thing I've ever had to an orgasm without any physical touching involved. It's succulent, savory, and should be illegal to sell. I close my eyes as I try to soak in the full experience. I go for another bite and the second wave of flavor smacks me again. I can feel my fork go up and down but at this point, I'm not controlling it. I hear "Hey!" I open my eyes and half the funnel cake is gone. Vorie is looking at me and she doesn't look very happy. I apologize for eating half of it, but it wasn't my fault that thing was so good. I fall back and I let her finish the rest of it because I know she wants it.

When she finished I ask her if she's ready to go find the ride tickets. She tells me yes and I help her clean up the table. We walk hand and hand looking for a ticket booth. We pass through the game section and Vorie gets distracted. "Donathan come on I have to play. This was my favorite carnival game growing up," she tells me. I follow her to this small pool of what looks like mechanical ducks. "Pick a duck! Any duck! You're a winner every time," yells the man working the game. I ask her what's the purpose of the game if you already know you're going to win. She responds to me, "It not about winning, it's about testing your luck." I reach into my pocket I give the man a $10 bill and he lets Vorie onto the platform. I watch her as she stares at the ducks go around and round. She picks up a pink one and flips it over. I can't see what it says from here but from her reaction I can tell she won big. I mean the man has already said everyone's a winner, so I don't know whether to join her in her joy or what. He takes the duck from her and screams "L for large, you must be really lucky. You can have any prize you want." She looks at the enormous stuffed animals surrounding the game and chooses a huge sea turtle. She brings it over to me and I take it from her because they're the same size. We continue on our journey for these tickets.

As we're aimlessly walking I'm looking at all the families that we're passing. These beautiful couples and young families, I wanted that. This young boy cuts in front of me dribbling a basketball. He can't be anything over 3. I almost trip carrying this gorilla turtle. He turns back to me and says, "Excuse me Mr." I go to say something back to the kid and I'm stuck in my tracks. He looks like me. I grab Vorie's arm and try to get her to turn around in time. "That little boy looked like me V," I say to her, but when I try to point him out to her he's already gone. Of course, she thinks I'm exaggerating and pulls me to keep walking. Seeing that little boy makes me think what life would have been like if we'd had a child. She wanted one and I told her that I wasn't ready. I wanted to propose to her first before we seriously talked about kids. I've been struggling to build up the courage, but I thought I had time to work on that. Silly me to think that we had all the time in the world.

We turn the corner and we've made it. We get in line at the ticket booth and I ask if the Ferris wheel

is all she wants to ride. To my surprise she says yes.
This is one of the quickest responses I've ever gotten
from this woman. I make my way to the front of the
line and buy two Ferris wheel tickets.

Walking out the line I hand her a ticket. Due to
the Ferris wheel being the tallest thing at this
carnival we have no problem finding our way to it. We
get in at the end of the line and the line starts to move
forward. I pray this line can speed up a little because
this turtle is getting heavy. I ask Vorie why'd she
even put this one on the list. She replies that she's
always wanted to feel like she was getting a kiss on
top of the world. Now this makes no sense to me, but I
love her, so I'll play along if it makes her happy.

We get to the front of the ride and the
attendant asks for our tickets. We give them to him
and wait for him to bring an empty cart around. One
lands in front of us and he catches it from swaying
back too far. Unhooking the door he opens the ride for
us. I take a step back and hold out my arm ushering
Vorie to go in first.

Vorie

I take Donathan's hand as I step into the
ride. Taking a seat on the bench I begin to scoot over
so he can have a seat. He takes my huge sea turtle
and sits him across from us. After scooting into the
ride the attendant closes the door behind him. The
ride starts and we slowly begin our cycle.

Every time we get to the top I love looking at
the view of the city. From up here, everything makes
you feel like you're a giant. When it comes to I would
say our third time going around the ride stops at the
top. Donathan puts his arm around me and asks how
have I been enjoying our day. "So far it's actually been
great sweetie. It feels good to spend this much time
with you," I confess. I scoot in closer so I can lean
under him. He agrees that today has been amazing,
but it shouldn't have taken what today might be to get
us to do it. Work isn't an excuse to put anybody off.
We make time for each other as much as we can, but
we should've been more aggressive about it. I start to

feel a little regret as we continue to talk about things, but it's too late for all that now.

My mind is going a thousand miles a minute right now and I want it to stop. I grab Donathan's face and I kiss him. We've been together for almost two years and his kisses still give me butterflies. We share a long passionate embrace then he backs away from me. "What was that for?" he asks. I proclaim that I'm fulfilling a dream. He stares into my eyes for a long time before he says anything else. "You know I wanted to marry you right?" he asks me. I let out a long sigh and nod my head yes. We thought we had time to save and plan for the perfect wedding. Now that seems like such an insignificant reason to be holding out on making our vows to each other. He kisses me again and again and again. My insides feel like a flower coming into its blossom. I stop and let our foreheads touch. He says to me, "On earth and in heaven we are bound V. It's just us." I throw my arms around his neck and hug him. I got lucky with this man.

I bring my mouth up to his ear and whisper to him, "I notice we've been up here for a pretty long time. What did you do?" I can feel him smile up against my cheek and he tells me he slipped the guy an extra thirty dollars to give us ten minutes alone. I sit back and laugh at him because I want to be surprised I really do but I know him very well and that's such a him thing to do. He sticks his hand over the ride and gives a thumbs up. The ride is moving again, and I have no words. I look at this man in amazement, even with the world possibly ending he's still unchanging.

We make it to the bottom and the ride comes to a stop. The attendant opens the door and these two shake hands. I can't handle him anymore, so I start pushing him out of the ride. He giggles as he climbs out. Taking his hand as he reaches back to help me, I climb out of the ride. He picks up my sea turtle and we start to walk toward the front.

As we're hand in hand a man calls out to Donathan. "Hey young man, you look like you've played a basketball game or two," he said. I let out a hefty sigh because I know of the monster that he has unleashed. Like a soldier, he does an about face and just like that he's sucked in. Donathan is very competitive and yes he used to play basketball. I can already play out the future of how this is going to go in my head, so I follow him and make myself comfortable on a bench nearby. I can hear the worker tell him he should win me a prize on his own and stop carrying around the one he knows I won for myself. I don't know if that's a tactic or if he works this carnival well enough to know that, but I know for sure he shouldn't have said it. Donathan ask him how much. The guy points to a sign that reads one ball for $5 or three for $10. Donathan asks him did he want to make things interesting and knowing men he was going to fall right into the trap. He says yes and I slap my forehead. Father forgive him for he not knowith the damages he bringith forth. Donathan tempts him to take part in a "friendly" wager. He agrees to pay Don out of pocket $5 for every 3 shots he makes in a row and for every 2 shots he misses he'll pay up $5. Now I won't say the guy's dumb for making the bet because it sounds good in theory. I sit back and watch it all unfold.

He gives him the first $10 bill and takes three balls. He misses the first two shots and makes the last one. Looking back at me he gives a very dramatic "Aaaaawwww Mannnnnnn!" and I can't contain my laughter. He takes out $5 and places it on the platform. The dudes face lights up when he sees that Donathan was legit about the money. Feeling confident he asks if he'd like another try. Donathan says yes and the rest is history.

I sit on this bench for the next twenty minutes watching as Donathan gives this guy the same pattern. Miss. Miss. Make. Miss. Miss. Make. These two have been going on so long that the stack that was once a lone $5 bill is now $50 dollars. People gather around to look on at the festivities and I know that will only make this sweeter for Donathan. Other men around him have started making bets on and against him. He continues to stay focused and deliver his pattern.

The bet is now up to $75. Donathan says out loud that this will be his last round because his pockets are getting low. The guy looks more than happy to go one more round. "Since this is the last round do you care to make this round more interesting," Donathan asks. The guy looks like he's

123

contemplating the thought and the men around him are pumping him up to do it so of course he agrees. Donathan tells him to pick up a collection from the audience and the final amount the loser has to match. "A double or nothing of sorts." He says with a smirk. The young worker takes off his hat and starts collecting money from those surrounding us. At this point, I am honestly shocked he's made it this far in his plan.

After everything was collected I walked over and counted the money as a whole. I'm holding $200 in my hand. The attendant rolls him three basketballs. Before he even picks one up Donathan asks him if he is sure this is what he wants. They shake on it and lock in the agreement. Donathan takes each ball and follows through with a perfect shot each time. The crowd around us gasp, I hold my head down in shame, the young man's hand covers his mouth, and Donathan has this look of fake surprise. Everyone is astonished by what happened. Donathan says, "Wow dude who could've known." I hold my breath because I know if I let this laugh out it'll come out as a yelp. People start to disperse from around us.

The guy is standing in sort of a stuck position. I snap my fingers in front of his eyes and it shakes him out of this trance he's in. "That'll be $200," Donathan tells him. Depressingly the guy reaches into his wallet and pulls out the money. He hands the money over. Donathan takes it plus the money that's still in my hand and tells him it was nice doing business with him.

Donathan picks up my sea turtle and we start our walk back to the car. "Why'd you do him like that," I ask him as we walk out the entrance. "Look he called me over there. Maybe he'll think twice next time he tries to sucker a dude in front of his girlfriend," he responds.

We make it to the car and Donathan puts my new son in the backseat. He comes over to open the door for me. Before closing it he bends down to kiss me on the cheek. By the time my brain can produce a response he's already gotten in the car. "Where to baby girl? I want to do something adventurous again," he says. Jokingly, I say so the horses weren't enough for you and he gives me a strong side-eye. I take out the list and scan it for any "adventurous" things.

"There's only one more thing we can do Mr. Badass," I say. He asks what that might be, and I tell him Paintball Precision. "Say less" is all he can get out before the car's pulling off.

Donathan

We pull up to Paint Precision and I can
already feel my blood pumping. I've always wanted to
have a paintball gun but Vorie would never let me
bring it in the apartment. This is the next best thing.
We get out of the car and head toward the store.

I open the door for Vorie, and we walk in
already looking around. There are guns lining the
walls, racks of safety vests, and target posters
everywhere. We walk toward the front and there is a
case full of color coated paintballs. "How may I help
you?" the guy behind the counter asked us. I let him
know that we're here to shoot on the obstacle course.
He asks if either one of us has ever fired a paintball
gun before.

I have the mind to lie and say yes but Vorie has
already answered no for us. He gives us the
opportunity to go do some practice rounds in the back.
I'm skeptical but if this is going to be my first time
I've got to go all out. We take him up on his offer and
he escorts us to a back room. It's kind of dark and my

senses are on high alert. Giving us two fully loaded paintball guns he goes behind the barricade to put up our posters. "Baby look how cool this is," Vorie says as the points the gun at me. I drop to the floor in defense. "Are you crazy," I yell at her from the ground. I've never seen this girl handle a gun before, so I definitely don't trust her pointing one at my chest. "Oh calm down I know what I'm doing," she replies. It's something about the tone of her voice that makes me get up a little slower.

He comes back to seeing me get off the floor and now I'm embarrassed. "You okay?" he questioned. I hurry to get up and convince him I'm fine. He tells us everything's ready for us to start our practice and to come to the front once we've had enough. On his way out he cuts on a light that brightens the area where our posters are hanging up. I take a stance in the first shooting lane and Vorie lines up next to me. With no hesitation, I hear her start to shoot. I jump because again I've never seen this woman handle any kind of firearm. I, on the other hand, have never shot at anything in my life. Handgun, paintball gun, water gun, none of that. I try to play it cool, and I hold the gun up to my shoulder. This is how I've seen others do it on YouTube. I look through the viewfinder, find the poster, and pull the trigger.

My first shot goes no where near my poster. So much for faking it until I made it. Even though I'm pretty sure she can answer her own question Vorie ask me if I've ever handled a gun before. I don't even dignify that with a verbal response, I continue to look at the floor. She laughs a little and takes the gun out my hand. After fixing my stance, she positions the paintball gun in my hand the way that it's supposed to be. I'd never thought I'd see the day where my baby would be giving me a tutorial on how to handle a gun.

She teaches me how to hold it steady and look through the view finder. I learn how to follow through with my shot and not shoot out of control. We spend at least a couple of minutes getting my shot to be something we could call decent. I inform her I'm ready to take this outside. She opens her eyes wide and says, "Are you sure about that Don?" I know I'm not the best, but I believe in my skills enough to go and not get taken out in the first five minutes. I shake my head matter of fact like and walk over to put my gun up. Vorie follows my lead and we start to walk back to the front.

When the guy behind the counter sees us he asks if we're ready for the big leagues. "Most definitely," I say as Vorie pinches me in the back. He tells us that there's a team outside missing two members if we wanted to join an actual paintball war team. He must've seen my killer skills to offer us this opportunity. I proclaim we'll do it before Vorie even can open her mouth. I take out my wallet and pay for us to join the thirty-minute war. He escorts us to the back where the rest of the group is getting ready.

We walk out the door leading to the back patio and there stands a group of ten people. Men and women getting dressed in a sea of camo. A woman comes up to us and introduces herself as the team captain. Zorrah reaches out to shake both of our hands. She tells us that they are an adult paintball war league. I happily ask if we may join them and she doesn't hesitate to say yes. She points in the direction of the protective suits and we waste no time in walking over.

We walk up to this rack of suits. Finding our sizes, we fall in line and start putting our things down to get dressed. Zorrah gets up in front of the group and let's everyone know they have some new players participating today. She gestures for us to come and stand in front of everyone. Shyly we get up and make our way in front of the flock. I introduce us as a couple. Zorrah tells everyone that this is our first time playing with the big dogs so take it easy on us. I was confident before but the way that they're looking at us now is making me unnerved. She asks if we have any questions and my hand goes up. "Will we feel the bullets with this protective gear on," I ask. I swear sometimes I can ask some pretty dumb things. I hear a couple of snickers, but nobody immediately answers my questions. Zorrah is staring at me as if for me to confirm that I'm serious about my question. Instead of giving me a useful answer she tells me I'll find out soon enough. I hate when people never flat out answer your question. She asks if everyone is ready to get out there and get going. The whole group around us cheers and I join in the festivities.

As a group, we walk to the meeting point of the paintball course. There are two boxes up in front with two different team colors. We're toward the back of the line. Babe, this is going to be fun," Vorie tells me. I can't lie and act as if I'm not as excited as she is. It's our turn now and we both grab a gun out of the same box. The woman behind us taps me on my shoulder. I turn around and she says, "Did we forget to tell you that we only play male against female." I look at Vorie to see how she feels about this and she doesn't budge. "Well I don't think that'll be a problem," I say as I hand the gun over to her. I reach back in and take the last gun out of the opposing box. I kiss Vorie and tell her I'll see her on the other side.

Walking over to the group of guys I shake their hands. They start to introduce themselves, but I hope they don't expect me to remember all their names. I ask one guy, "What's the game plan." He tells me they usually wing it. I look from face to face as the other guys nod in agreement. I force a smile and say, "Well this should be some interesting."

Vorie

I take my gun and follow the woman deeper into the field. Walking through the trees we come up on the other four women. When we reach them they're deep in strategy talk on how we're going to take on the guys. I'm hearing their plan, but I can't contribute because this is my first time doing something like this. Don't get me wrong I'm a strong shot, but that's only been with animals up until this point. "Vorie what do you think we should do," Zorrah asks me. Now I'm like a deer caught in headlights. "Honestly I was planning on following you," I respond back. Everyone else turns their head to look at her reaction like I've said something wrong. "We don't have to worry about your loyalty do we Vorie," she asks me. Last time I checked this was a game. I'm getting interrogated like I'm on the stand. "No, you don't have to worry about me," I assure.

An announcer comes onto a loudspeaker somewhere and starts to give us the rules of the game. He tells us that they have cameras everywhere out here so there will be no way for anyone to cheat. Once someone is shot he will come back on and announce it to everyone. He warns us to be safe and to not hurt ourselves running or shooting. When he's done giving us his speech there's a horn that starts blaring loud. It rings three times and I'm guessing that's the start of the game.

On command the women all crouch down and start to pace the grounds. I follow their leads. Zorrah gives up a hand signal and I have no idea what it means. In an instant the woman in front of me whispers back, "Keep your ears open."

We're making our way in a huge circle and all of a sudden we hear a branch snap. For some reason my heart starts beating heavy. I know this a game, and nothing will happen to me but being out in the open and exposed that's freaking me out. That thought doesn't cross your mind until it's you who's being hunted. As a group, we lower to the ground and Zorrah throws up another sign that I'm told translates to "be looking around". Arising from our right, a guy jumps out from behind a bush and before his feet even make it to the ground he's sprayed. The mysterious voice comes back through the speaker and says, "5 guys left." We continue to move forward, and he lays there on the ground. Now I'm confused on if we're supposed to play dead or get up and walk away if we're shot. I go to ask, and someone interrupts me to say that we should split up. With no discussion three women walk away in a different direction. I'm left with Zorrah and some girl who's name I don't know. We start walking along the left side of the trail and find ourselves behind a bush. We choose to stay undisclosed behind these shrubs until we see some movement. Off in the distance we hear two shots go off. The announcer comes on and says that there are only three guys left. "That's my girls," Zorrah whispers.

The woman bending next to me says that we should use her as bait. Before Zorrah or I can even respond she's already out in the open drawing attention to herself. Idiot. It's beyond the point of saying something so I pull my gun out and get ready to shoot. Just as suspected two men come out from behind the trees. We let them come close enough to draw out their weapons and we both shoot.

137

The announcer comes on to say that there is only one man left. Zorrah pats me on the back for my shot. We come from behind the bush and go meet bait girl. They put their hands around their mouths and let out this weird calling sound. A few seconds and the other women come from out of the trees behind us. We all gather together and throw around ideas on how we plan to take down this last man. I'm listening with my ears but in my mind, I'm praying it's not Donathan. When I mentally tap back into the conversation they've already decided to zero in on him. We break out our formation and form a perimeter circle around the entire field. Step by step we move in closer to the center.

I spot what appears to be in the fetal position on the ground a ways in front of me the last man. Now would be a good time to know their hand signals. I start jumping and pointing in the direction I see him. I see a couple of thumbs up through the greenery, so I know that my message is being received. He's down with his back turned to me so he would've been an easy target, but I wanted to get a closer shot. Oh my gosh, who am I becoming. Easing toward him I try not to make a sound. I see I'm the closest one to him, so I know I'll be the one to take the shot. I'm less than 30 yards away and I hear a snap. I look down and see that I've brought my foot down on a long branch. I look up to see him quickly swivel in my direction. I look past him, and everyone is frozen still waiting for his reaction with their hand on their guns. I wait for him to make a move on me and he doesn't. I take my gun from my side and position myself to take the shot. He's just standing there looking at me not doing anything. I don't want to shoot a man that's not even trying to protect himself.

We have this stand off for God knows how long. I see his hand flinch and that's enough for me to take the shot. The announcer comes on one final time to say that the women have come out victorious. The women start to jump and celebrate our win. I walk over to the man I shot in the chest and take his helmet off. Donathan stands in front of me with a Cheshire cat grin. "I knew it was you," I announce. He starts to laugh. I ask him why he didn't shoot so the game could be over. "Come on now you know I could never shoot at you, even if it was fake. Plus, I could feel your posse wasn't too far away. I'd rather take your one bullet against their five," he replies. He grabs my face and kisses me. With no fight left in me I give in and kiss back.

Hand in hand we follow the rest of the group back to the patio. When we arrive back the men are already changed and waiting on us. "How'd you end up the last man standing," says one of the guys from the table. "I guess I'm a lucky man," Donathan responds as he puts his arm around me. Zorrah comes over and thanks us for playing with them. "Anytime you want to come and shoot like that you are more than welcome," she says. I smile and thank her for letting us be a part of their team for the day. We walk over to the bin where everyone was putting their emptied guns and we add ours to the pile. Walking over to our things, I check my phone. "Honey, it's almost 4:45," I say at him. He looks at me like I'm retarded. "We're almost late to our next activity," I explain further.

We take off our paintball suits and hang them up on the used rack. We pick up our belongings and wave bye to everyone as we pass them on the way to the door. Going through the building, the man behind the counter yells after us to come back again anytime.

Donathan opens the door for me and says, "You're rushing like you have an idea of where you want to go." I disclose I have something in particular that I wanted to save until after we did something that he wanted to do. Of course, he starts bombarding me with questions and I hold my hand out waiting on the keys. He rolls his eyes as he reaches in his pocket to give them to me. I unlock the car and tell him to get in as I jog around to the driver's seat.

Donathan

We pull up to a shopping center. I'm looking at the business names on the street sign to see where we could be going. We pass storefronts and none of them look to be something either one of us would put on our list. She pulls into a parking spot in front of a store window and I see that I was mistaking. Sunrise Tattoos. I put my head in my hands. This girl has brought me to a tattoo shop. "Are you serious dude?" I ask her. She doesn't even respond to me. She gets out the car and walks toward the entrance. Unwillingly I get out the car and follow her into the shop.

We get to the counter and a very tattooed individual comes from the back. "How may I help you two today," he asks as he starts to take off some medical gloves. My stomach drops to my toes. Vorie tells him that we would like to be walk ins today. He grins as he looks at me. As if he can smell my fear from right where I stand. He asks for our ID's and if we have ideas of what we want. Vorie looks at me as if I'm supposed to say what we plan on getting. My face twists up and I look at her. Her logic sometimes baffles me. I tell him that we don't have any ideas at the moment. In that second I wish I hadn't said anything because I heard how my voice cracked. This place has me shaken up. He points to the walls behind us and instructs us to go look at some stencils while he makes copies of our ID's.

As we walk across the room Vorie asks me is there something I'd like us to get. "Stop acting like I'm the one that put this on our list. I know it was you woman," I say. She gives me this guilty smile. "So, you really don't want to do this," she asks me. Now I have no choice but to go through with this. I can't say I'm scared of needles and watch her get something. I'm a man and I can overcome this stupid fear. I agree to go through it but only if she'll let me get something small.

The guy comes over to bring us our ID's and ask if we'd made our final decision yet. I quickly tell him no. He tells us he'll attend to us after he finishes with his customer in the back. He finally introduces himself as Odin.

We start to flip through these tattoo boards that are on the wall. I'm seeing these huge art pieces and there is no way that I would ever get anything this size. As I flip through toward that back the sizes start to get smaller and I start to get a little comfortable in this realm. Vorie's flipping through the boards next to me and ask how I feel about getting something that matches. I hadn't thought about that, but I agree to it only because this will be my first and last tattoo no matter what the outcome of tomorrow is.

In the politest way, I make sure she understands I won't be getting anything bigger than a business card. We continue to flip through these boards, but nothing is standing out to either of us. I walk over to a new set of boards and she follows me. I start looking at these and they're more designs of hearts and love. They're more feminine than I'd want on my body but I'm starting to like these.

As we get toward the end of the boards, the drawings turn into couple tattoo designs. I look back at Vorie to confirm this is what she wants, and she shakes her head happily. Getting to the last board, I think I've found it. His Last. Her Forever. It's perfect.

147

She says I'm leaning more toward this one and points
to the one that I'm in love with. I reply I like it too
and she starts acting all dramatic. "Oh, this must be
the one if you're saying that you like it too," she says.
I roll my eyes and go sit in the waiting area. She
comes over and plops down next to me. "Do you think
it's going to hurt sweetheart," she asks. Up until now
I was only thinking about the needle being involved. I
never thought about how it would feel. My hands
begin to sweat. I try to wipe my hands on my pants
where she won't notice but of course the woman I
have does. She grabs my hand and apologizes for
making me nervous.

Odin walks to the front with the customer that
he was previously working on. His leg's wrapped but I
can still see the blood dripping from his tattoo. I had
no idea that getting a tattoo could make you bleed. My
palm's go from a light drizzle to a category five
hurricane. They exchange a few words then the guy
leaves. Odin walks over to us and ask what is the
decision we've made. Vorie gets up and takes him over
to the board we chose and shows him what we want.
In my mind I got up with them, but my knees are

locked in the same place. He tells us he'll go to the back and draw out the stencils. He disappears to the back and this would be the perfect time to escape. We haven't paid anything, and the front door is right there. When Vorie comes back to sit next to me I plan to bring up my genius plan to her.

As my mouth delays to open I hear, "So where do you want to put them?" My insides get all tingly. "I don't know. Where to you think would hurt less," I ask. I realize I've dug myself deeper into this hole. She suggests the wrist and I'm a little skeptical. I would think the wrist would hurt because there's veins right there. "Are you sure Vorie," I ask and very confidently she says yes. Odin comes to the front and tells us that he's ready.

I see Vorie walking away from me, but my body doesn't register that it's time for me to get up. I put both hands on the sides of this seat and I push myself up. I follow both of them into the back room. We push past a curtain and there the chair is. "I have to go to the bathroom," I yell out. They both look at me like I'm crazy and Odin points in the direction of the bathroom. I speed walk away and lock myself up in the bathroom. I caught a glimpse of what I look like in the mirror and I can say that this is not my best. I'm pale, sweaty, and shaking. I look at myself and give me a pep talk.

> - *"You are not scared. Go out there and man up. Do you see Vorie out there on the verge of tears? No, you don't! You're going to go out there and take a seat in that chair and go first. You're not going to hold her hand and you're not going to flinch."*

I don't know if I believe myself completely, but it's enough to put on brave face and go back out there.

I walk out and Vorie is talking to Odin about the size of the tattoo. They notice I come back, and he asks which one of us would like to go first. Vorie looks at me waiting on my answer. I can't make out her facial expression, so I don't know if she wants me to volunteer first. I take a deep breath with every intention of saying me, but my finger beats my mouth and points at her.

Vorie

I knew he was going to do that to me. I
shake my head as a take a seat in the tattoo chair.
He's lucky I'm not as scared as he is because I
would've definitely made him sit through this first.
Donathan takes a seat in the chair against the wall.
Odin starts pouring black ink into these miniature
cups. "Will you hold my hand Don," I ask Donathan. I
decide no matter how this feels I'm going to act like
it's the most painful thing ever. That'll teach him. He
agrees to hold my hand and I know this is going to
mess up his nerves up even more.

Odin sticks the needle in the gun and starts
testing the equipment. When I start to hear that
sound up close my stomach jumps a little. Okay I am
a little nervous but I'm not going to be a baby about it.
One of us has to be the strong one. Odin ask me to
hand him my wrist so he can put the stencil on. I turn
over my left wrist and he put this thin piece of paper
on it. He takes it off and the words are there. His
Forever. I'm about to get this put on my body. Odin

151

ask if the positioning is right before he starts, and I say yes. Instantly I reach for Donathan's hand and he gives it to me.

I look away from my arm because I didn't want to see but I felt that bad boy. The needle goes onto my skin and I tense up. I don't cry out in pain but it's a steady sting that I'm feeling right now. I tighten my grip on his hand. Placing my other hand on my thigh, involuntarily it starts to grasp for help. Odin looks up to ask if I'm okay and I nod quickly up and down. I'm afraid if I break my concentration then I'll let a tear slip.

As quickly as he starts he's finished. Odin whips my arm with a napkin and covers my tattoo with some sort of clear gel. "Do you want to see it now or would you like to wait until he gets his," he asks me. I opt out to wait for my boo. He takes some clear wrap and wraps it around my wrist. I get up out the chair and I show Donathan what it looks like with the wrap on it. "I don't want to look at it yet Don but what do you think," I ask. He tells me that it's almost as beautiful as I am. I start to blush.

Odin starts to wipe the chair down and clean up so that Donathan can go next. When he sees this, he announces that he has to go to the bathroom again. I swear I could kill him sometimes. I apologize to Odin for his behavior and he tells me a lot of first timers are way worse than him so it's fine. I watch him change the needles and ink thinking I wish I was an artist like this.

He comes back from the bathroom and sits in his original seat. "Babe it's your turn to sit in the big chair," I inform him. He acts like he doesn't hear me. I sit on the edge of this wide chair and physically push him up. He plops from chair to chair and now he's in the hot seat. Odin puts his hand on Donathan's shoulder and tries to lean him back. "You can get comfortable if you'd like," he tells him. Like a sheet of metal Don leans back stiff. Odin grabs his wrist and puts the stencil on. I reach out and grab his hand because I know he'll need that. He squeezes back and I know he feels me here. Odin ask him if he's ready to get things started and with his voice shaking he says yes.

When the needle first touches his skin, he does a killer grip on my hand. I want to scream at him to loosen up, but I don't want him to move and mess up the tattoo. This hurts more than actually getting the tattoo. He stares straight forward at the wall and I now he's trying to put on a brave face. I start to rub my thumb over his knuckles because I know that soothes him. Odin takes a break to turn around and get more ink and Donathan tries to get up. "What are you doing sweetie," I ask him. He looks like his heart breaks when he sees he has a little more left to go.

Odin jumps right back in there and finishes up Donathan's tattoo. He tells Don to look down at his arm. When I say this dude's whole mood changed, I was astonished myself. "Oh, that's clean man thank you," he says while smiling. He goes to touch it and Odin pops his hand. "Don't touch it with your dirty hands. You could mess it up," he says. I cover my mouth and try not to laugh at how sad Donathan looks right now. He cleans the tattoo up and wraps it like he did mine.

Donathan gets out the chair and we walk up to the mirror together. We hold our wrist out and examine our tattoos next to each other. "Not half bad baby," he says, and I can't help but to feel warm inside. After cleaning up his area Odin comes over and ask how we like them. I voice we couldn't be any happier with the results. He escorts us to the front. Donathan pulls out his wallet and pays for our new artwork.

Donathan opens the door for me as we walk out the tattoo shop. We make it to the car, and I get in. He cuts the car on and looks at me. "Where to Ma'am," he asks me. I take out our list. I'm looking at the things we have left, and I can't decide on where we should go. I close my eyes and point somewhere. When I open my eyes I see my finger is on roller skating. My heart sinks because I don't know how to skate, nor do I have the desire to learn today. "What'd you pick babe," Donathan ask me as he leans over the armrest. He sees my finger is on roller skating and he gets more excited then he's been for anything today. "Skating?! Hecks yeah, I know the place to go" he says as he puts the gear shift in drive.

Donathan

We pull up to the skating ring and luckily the parking lot isn't that packed for a Saturday afternoon. I get out the car and start walking toward the front door. I haven't been skating in so long and this is Vorie's first time so I'm very excited. I get halfway to the door when I realize this girl is still sitting in the car. I turn around and jog back to the car. I knock on the window and that happens to snap her out of whatever trance she's in. I open the door for her. "You okay sweetie," I ask. She tells me that she's fine, but I don't believe that for a second. We walk hand in hand to the entrance.

I open the door for her, and we walk-in. Even with not being here in over seven years everything still looks the same. The chipped paint and outdated carpet make me feel right at home. I walk us over to the front counter. "Hi, how may I help you today," the person behind the counter ask me. I read his name tag and say, "Yes Wilder I'd like to get two skaters' tickets and a locker." He rings me up and hands over the tickets with a key. I nod my head at him and take the items.

"Why don't we get the skates from the front," Vorie ask me as we walk into the actually skating rink. I try to explain to her that you pay for the ticket and then take that to the skate check out and that's where you get them. I have no good reason to give on why they do things like that, it's how it's always been.

We approach the desk and I can't believe my eyes. "Is that the infamous Remington," I say to the man with his back turned to us tightening a pair of skates. He turns around and his eyes light up. "Donathan," he says with a questioning look on his face. We reach across the counter and shake hands. I introduce Vorie to the man that taught me everything I know about skating. "Nice to meet you," she says as he reaches to shake her hand.

We spend a minute catching up because it's been so long. "Came here to knock the old dust off your feet I see," he tells me. I think to say something that would sound more normal but instead I tell the truth. I tell Remington about the email and about what we are doing with our last day on earth. To my surprise he

confides in us that he got the email this morning too. I
ask him if he believes it and he tells me yes. "If you
know this is your last day on earth why aren't you out
doing something," I ask him. "Edith and I lived each
day like it was our last and when I lost her two years
ago I lost my world. Every day since then I've woken
up praying that this is the day we meet again. My
prayers finally have been answered, I don't want
anything but for tomorrow to come faster," he
explains to me. I can't help but to smile and reach
over to grab his hand. I remember growing up coming
here every weekend and seeing him and his wife here.
They were a couple that I admired as a young man.
Their love was definitely one made for movie screens.
"I didn't know that she passed Rem, I'm so sorry," I
say. He tells me not to worry about it, he'll be seeing
his leading lady first thing in the morning. We laugh
together and I find myself admiring this man just like
I did when I was a young boy. To have that mind set
is not something common and very mature. "Enough
of the sob stuff what size skates does the little lady
need," he asks as he turns his attention toward Vorie.
She blushes and ask for a size eight. Disappearing

161

behind the racks of skates, he comes back with two matching black pairs. "Still remember my size old man," I joke as I take the skates from him. He wags his finger at me and says, "I got your old man."

I bring Vorie over to the benches by the lockers and we take a seat. I hand over her skates and start to unlace my shoes. I look over and she's still holding the skates in her lap. Before I can get out are you okay she confesses to me that she's terrified of skating. My mouth drops and I ask her why she didn't tell me. "You were so excited, and I didn't want to disappoint you," she tells me. Now I feel like an idiot for not noticing how nervous she was acting. "Vorie we didn't have to come here. We could've did something that we both wanted to do. This day is about spending time together not just about me," I tell her. She tells me that if I can face my fear of needles and get a tattoo for her then she can fall on her face for me. I lean over and kiss her because this girl is nothing short of amazing. I get up and sit on the ground at her feet. Taking her shoes off I help her learn how to put the skates on. I strap them up for her and she helps me stand up. I sit back down next to her and bend over to put my own skates on.

"Let me go put our things in the locker before we go out there," I announce. She hands me her purse and I skate over to the locker. Locking our things up I skate back over to her and ask if she's ready. She gives me a very uneasy look, but I ensure her things are going to be fine. I take both her hands and try to help her stand up. She barely can get up a few centimeters before her feet fly from under her. Fortunately, we hadn't gone anywhere yet. "Honey, you have to stand up," I urge her trying not to laugh. She snaps her neck up to me at lightning speed and my laughter intensifies.

We start over again and I get her up on her feet. I guide her as slow as possible to the skating ring. We get to the perimeter of the rink where we have to step down. To avoid her landing on her face I pick her up and step down for the both of us. I make sure her footing is good before I let go. Her hands shoot up and grab the railing.

I stand in front of her and try to give her a verbal lesson on how to skate. I can tell from her facial expression that this method isn't working. "Give me your hands and I'm going to hold onto them while we go around," I instruct her. She's never cussed me out before but from the twitch of her upper lip she almost broke her all-time record. I advise her to trust me. She quickly transfers her hands from the railing to my forearms. Her nails go into my skin and I bite my lip in an attempt to not yelp out in pain.

"I'm going to skate backwards, and I want you to slowly come toward me. If you fall I will catch you. I'm right here," I say to her. I start to move backwards at a slow pace and try to pull her along. We take off at a snail pace around the rink. With each lap we take I speed up a little more. She starts to get the hang of things and I ask her if she wants me at her side. Her face is telling me heck no, but she says yes. I grab her hand and we start to go around again. I'm so proud of her for learning so fast. "You're doing great babe," I encourage. She smiles and I can tell she's actually having a great time.

"Let go Don," she tells me. I'm kind of stunned that she's requesting this, so I ask her to make sure I heard right. "You sure you want that sweetie," I ask.

She tells me I said it myself that she's going great. Well she's got a point I did say that. I let go of her hand and watch her skate away from me. She's doing amazing to consider where she started from twenty minutes ago.

She's on the other side of the rink now. I give her a thumbs up, so she knows I'm still watching. She goes to lift up her hands to give me two thumbs back and my worst fears don't let me down. In slow motion I see her legs go back and her face come forward. I try to cover my eyes because I can't bear to watch what's about to happen. I don't see it, but you can believe I heard it. I uncover my eyes and she's on the ground face down.

Vorie

My face hurts. I can't see anything, and my face freaking hurts. One minute I was skating fine and now my face feels terrible. I feel somebody touching me and it's a little easier for me to see. I see Donathan now and I'm a little less panicked. "Babe are you ok," I hear him ask. Trying to sit up from the ground, a gush of liquid come down my face. I touch where is wet and its red. My eyes widen and I look up at Donathan. I'm bleeding. I must have hit my head pretty bad because I start laughing. He's now looking at me like I have completely lost my mind. "Sweetie we have to go clean your face," he tells me. I shake my head ok and he begins to take my skates off.

With skates in one hand and me in the other Donathan guides me off the skating rink. He puts me down and instructs me to hold my head back. I'm led to the bathroom and forced to sit down on the benches right outside the door. He goes to get tissue for me.

Coming back with a wad of tissue he stuffs it into my face. "I told you I couldn't skate," I say to him.

He never listens to me. Why would he choose today out of all days to start? I'm holding this tissue to my nose and I don't even know what condition it's in. Is it broken, split open, or cracked? Am I still beautiful? "Why did you listen to me," I ask him. I hear him chuckle. Twisting my head toward him I catch him laughing. I can't believe that he's laughing at me right now. "I'm sorry babe but you asked me to let you go. I thought you had it," he says. Okay I guess I did do this to myself and I can't blame him 100%. "I thought I had it too," I laugh.

I take the tissue from my nose because it's soaked, and he already has another wad ready to give me. I love this guy. I put the wad up to my nose and we sit by the bathroom.

After it feels like the blood has stopped pouring out my nose I go into the bathroom to clean it out. Seeing myself in the mirror for the first time, I looked like I had been hit by a bus. A heavy double decker to be exact. I wet some napkins and clean the blood from my nose. After it's all gone I try my best to fix up my hair and the rest of my face. When I come out the bathroom Donathan is standing by the door already

167

holding a bottled water for me. He gives me the bottle and we walk over to the benches where we were seated when we first got here. "Before we do anything else today you're going to sit here and drink this water," he tells me. I hate water but I know he's trying to take care of me. I sit and begin to sip.

As I'm drinking I look at the other skater's skate right past us. They look like they're having so much fun. Ages young to old all floating around together. Seeing everyone flowing on one accord inspires me. "I'm not leaving here until I get this down," I tell Donathan. He looks at me crazy and ask am I really trying to go out there again. I finish the water and hand him back the empty bottle. He knows me well enough to take that as my yes. Shaking his head at me he gets back on the floor to put my skates on for me one last time. Once they're on my confidence starts to fade a little but I have to catch myself. In that moment the phrase I live by pops in my head. Don't stray from the storm, learn how to sail through it. Today is my day to sail.

I'm up and he's guiding me back to rink. We get to the perimeter and it's time for me to step down.

Donathan goes to pick me up again and I order him not to. He backs up from me and I grab the railing myself and step down. Step 1 is complete. He comes back to my side and holds my hand. I don't think I'm going to let it go this time.

We start skating around the rink just like before. I actually enjoy it when we skate like this. We're in our own groove of things and Donathan ask me if I want to let go again. I know he's being sarcastic so with my free hand I punch him in the arm. He starts cracking up and I can admit I let out a laugh or two. I'm savoring these moments of us going around at our moderate pace, but a man can never be satisfied with simple. "Do you want to learn how to cross your feet?" he asks me. Now against my better judgement I say yes. He guides me over to the side. He shows me what he means by crossing my feet and I should've went with my first mind and said no.

I try for the first time and I can confidently say I did not look as smooth as he did at all. I was rough if I've ever seen it before. He giggles at me as he tries to help me get it down better. We practice for like fifteen minutes before I start to get the flow of things. After feeling myself in the groove I instruct him to step back and let me shine. Obviously not too far in case I face plant again. I start doing it on my own and when I look up I realize I've made it halfway around the rink. I start to look around to see where Donathan is and I remember that's what messed me up the first time. I calm down and let my body do its thing. My feet carry me through the motions, and I let the rest of my body follow. I block out my surroundings and just skate. I feel free as the wind passes me and I pick up speed.

As I'm finishing my circle Donathan finds himself next to me. He grabs my hand and our bodies go in sync. Our bodies are skating, our feet are crossing, and our heads are bobbing to the music. I'm so in the moment that nothing else matters. It's like we're the only two out here. Everyone else is boxed out.

A malicious roar comes from my stomach that shakes the earth with no warning. Donathan looks at me and I can't do anything but feel embarrassed. "You hungry," he asks me, and I shake my head yes. I was enjoying skating, but my stomach has spoken. He tells me that he's already got dinner covered and we make our way to the exit.

My gentleman boyfriend offers me his hand so he can help me out the rink. We skate over to where our locker is, and I take a seat. While I struggle to get these skates off he goes to get our things. Coming back he sees me still having issues unlacing my skates. He sits on the floor in front of me once more and helps me undo them. He places my regular shoes on my feet and makes sure they're straight before he gets up. I could get used to this pampering. Getting up he replaces his skates with his regular shoes.

We walk over to the counter and wait for Remington to come to the front. He comes from the back and ask me if I'm okay and my heart drops to the bottom of my backside. I had no idea that somebody saw me face surf on the rink. Donathan tries to answer for me but I'm so embarrassed I start pulling him toward the door. He gives way to me and they yell goodbye to each other from a distance.

Once we're outside he starts laughing at me. I try to change the subject and ask where we're going to eat. I get no answer. He opens the door for me so I can get in the car and I do. When he opens the driver's door to get in I ask him again where are we going eat. "Somewhere I know you'll love," is all I can get out of him before we're pulling off.

Donathan

We pull up to The Golden Dior and it's one of the biggest restaurants I've ever seen in person. We're in the valet line and Vorie says we aren't dressed for a place like this. "Nonsense love today is our day," I remind her. It's now our turn and the valet comes up to my door. He opens it for me, and I get out to go open Vorie's door. I stick out my hand and say, "Will you come with me Madam." She blushes but grabs my hand and gets out.

I lead her up this grand staircase. Once we get to the top there is a revolving front door. When we walk through it I gasp. This restaurant is so beautiful. I know the food is going to be beyond expensive but I'm proud to bring her here. I used to wine and dine Vorie when we began dating but I can admit over time I started to slack off. Tonight will be different though. I'll make tonight perfect.

I escort my date up to the podium in the front. "Last name," the waiter asks me. I confess that we don't have a reservation, but we'll sit anywhere. He gives me a displeased look and checks the book in front of him. "I'll be one moment," he says as he walks away from us. We stand here looking out of place as we wait from him to come back. "This was a last-minute plan," she asks me in a whisper. She knows me so well. "Why yes my darling it was," I reply.

On his return the waiter expresses that they only have one table available for the rest of the night. Letting out a deep breath, I tell him that we'll be taking that table. He escorts us through the restaurant until we come to a table set right next to the kitchen door. "This is the table," he tells us. It's not the most romantic location but at least we have somewhere to sit. I had no plan b if this didn't work out. He tells us he'll be back to take our drink order. Leaving us standing there he walks away. Definitely won't be getting a tip from me. I walk around to the other side of the table and gesture for Vorie to sit down. I push her chair in and take a seat myself. She starts unfolding her napkin to put in her lap and I can't help but see how she fits in this environment. I should've been taking her to places like this. Hands down I have the most stunning date in this whole building. "This is so nice my love. Thank you for bringing me," she tells me. I just smile because I'm so dumb struck by her beauty right now.

I pick up my menu and start to look at what they have to eat. Everything on this menu is in French. I should've looked that up before I brought her here. I'm looking through titles that look familiar but the only thing I'm getting is the restaurant's name. The waiter comes back and ask us what we'd like to drink. Vorie looks at me like she's waiting on me to respond. I confidently say we'll be having a bottle of Chateau for the night. The waiter looks a little stunned, but he nods and walks away.

Vorie leans across the table and whispers, "Can we afford to eat here?" I tell her if tomorrow is what we think it is then there is no reason not to treat ourselves to the finer things. "We'll be fine babe. I have the money," I assure her. She relaxes more and continues to look at her menu.

When the waiter comes back, he opens the bottle of wine right in front of us. Pouring both of our glasses, he places the remainder in a bucket of ice on the table. He takes out a notepad and ask if we would be indulging in any hors d'oeruves tonight. Now I start to scratch my head because this man expects me to know what the word hors d'oeruve means. I didn't want to be the uncultured dummy in the room, but I ask, "What is an hors d'oeruve?" He tells me that it's another word for appetizer and now I'm wondering why he didn't just start with that.

Scanning the menu I can't understand any of these names and the descriptions don't make things any better. I already feel out of place, so I don't want to ask him to explain each item to me. I eeny, meeny, miny, moe the hors d'oeruve column and my finger lands on Cocktail de Scampi. In my most prestigious voice I say, "We'll be having the Cocktail de Scampi with extra butter sauce please." He tells us that it will be on the way shortly and I'm surprised that I said it right. When he leaves Vorie asks me what exactly I ordered. "We'll find out when it comes out," I reply. She laughs at me and I ask her if she knows what she wants to order yet. Of course she tells me no. She can't read the menu any better than I can. I mention I'll leave her alone to google pictures of what's on the menu. That started as a joke, but I listen to my own advice. I take out my phone and get to googling.

Most of these things don't even look edible and the other half are served raw. Why do rich people eat so nasty? I get down to the last few things on the menu and I've come to a decent decision. When I look up to tell Vorie I can see that she is in deep thought over there. I laugh on the inside at the face that she's making. This woman sitting across from me is the love of my life. I was supposed to marry her. I was going to give her the home of her dreams. Kids. We wanted to have kids. Now that will never happen. A lump forms in my throat, and I try to push it back down. I've done a great job at keeping my emotions in check all day. I don't want to ruin the mood, so I keep my thoughts to myself.

I want to make this night special. I want tonight to exceed all other nights we've shared together. I want this moment to be the last one she thinks about until the end of our time. I didn't have anything planned but I know one thing I can do that will shake her up. I'm sick of living in fear. I've faced so much today, and I can take one more leap of faith.

The waiter comes back with a martini glass with shrimp surrounding the rim. My first instinct is to ask is this it, but I refrain myself from saying such things. He asks us will that be all for the moment. "Yes, thank you," I reply. When he walks away I stare at Vorie. I can see that she's holding her laughter in not wanting to draw attention toward us. Before I open my mouth to say anything I take a sip of the wine. At least we get a healthy portion of something around here. I offer her to take one first since this date is about me treating her. "You sure babe," she asks me. I push her to hurry and take one before I change my mind. Amused she reaches to the glass and takes a shrimp. I wait for her reaction before I take one. Taking a bite, her eyes retract into her head. I don't know rather to be alarmed or disgusted. "Sweetheart you have to try one," she says with her mouth full. I take a shrimp from the glass and dip it into the sauce inside the cup. From the moment I place the shrimp in my mouth it dissolves. "Oh my God," I say louder than expected. A few people from surrounding tables look over at us in distaste. Any other time I would've proceeded to ask them what they were looking at, but this shrimp has my tongue in knots.

We share the rest of what's in this small martini glass. That was the best miniature shrimp I've ever had the pleasure of consuming. I sit back in my chair trying to act like I'm fulfilled. If I act well enough my stomach will believe it. "That didn't do anything Don, I'm still starving," Vorie says to me. I'm convinced this girl can read my mind. I tell her my stomach is still touching my back and that wins a smile out of her. I reach over and grab her hand. Her cheeks pinken and she ask me what I want with her hand. I state that depends on what she'll agree to.

V⊕rie

Before I can ask Donathan what he means by that the waiter comes back. "Do you all know what you would like to order yet," he ask. Sitting here googling items on this menu, the only thing that looks appealing is the Pollo Alla Scarpariello. I place my order, and he tells me that is a good choice. Donathan orders a Fettuccine Alfredo and the waiter seems to be a little less impressed. I chuckle to myself because I know he's trying his hardest. He leaves with our orders and Donathan ask me if I'd like more wine. I say yes and he tops my glass off. I take a sip and over my rim I can see this man lift the bottle to his mouth.

I sit here looking astonished at what he just did in this elegant restaurant. "Babe are you okay? What has gotten into you?," I ask. He continues to drink from the bottle, and I start to notice the stares. I reach across the table and take the bottle from his mouth. What the heck is going on with this man? He starts to tell me he's sorry for not giving me the attention I deserve these past couple of months. I see

182

all the wine we've had is starting to catch up to him. "We already talked about this sweetie. I forgive you," I say. "But I told you it was because of work and I lied Vorie that wasn't it," he tells me fiddling with his fingers. I don't know what he's about to say but I don't want it to ruin our dinner. I demand he not tell me what it is. We've went this long with him keeping whatever it is a secret and he can take it with him to the grave. He keeps trying to explain himself, but I don't want to hear it. I refuse to go into the next couple of hours upset and alone so he can clear his conscience. In the mist of me going back and forth with him he starts to get louder with me. I don't want to argue with him, so I try to reason that this is not the place to cause a scene. The last thing I wanted to do was get into an argument today.

Before I can say my next line Donathan says, "Marry me." At first I'm not sure I'm hearing correctly, so I ask him to repeat himself. Like I thought he said the first time, I hear marry me. I fix my mouth to let something come out but just like that the waiter is back with our food.

183

He sets the plates down and ask can he do anything else for us. I'm still looking into Donathan's eyes and he's still looking into mine. I want to look away but it's like I'm being hypnotized. This man asked me to marry him. After seeing he wasn't going to get an answer the waiter walked away. Donathan reaches for my hand and ask me once more to marry him. I'm trying to wrap my head around this. Where is this even coming from? I ask him if he's serious and he tells me he's never been more serious about anything. He starts explaining to me that this is why he's been acting distant toward me. He's been waiting for the perfect time to ask me for a while now and with the added pressures of today as our clock counts down it was either now or never. "Where are we going to get married at eight o'clock at night on a Saturday? You don't even have a ring," I announce. I don't mean to be rude, but he can't be serious right now.

He has this genius plan to go to a 24-hour chapel and get married. "We can pick up a ring on the way my queen," he tells me. I give him a look of uncertainty. Yes, I love him but a quickie wedding? He can see that I'm not completely sold on the idea, so he keeps giving me selling points. "I do not want to leave this earth without you as my wife Vorie," he tells me. I was driving a hard bargain, but he's starting to wear me down. He explains to me he thought he had to make everything perfect before he could ask me. With today being what it could, he realizes all we needed was us and our love. "So, what do you say V, will you marry me, tonight," he asks. I don't think about anything and I decide to go with my heart. I tell him yes and I can see the relief on his face. Being his wife is what I've wanted for a long time and the end of the world isn't going to stop any of that.

He walks around to my side of the table and kisses me passionately. I'm so happy right now I can hardly contain my excitement. I'm getting married! I rush him to go back to his side of the table because our food is getting cold. He gives me one last kiss before he goes and sits down.

We start to eat, and I can't even engage in conversation because I have so many thoughts on my mind. If you would've told me this morning when I woke up on the floor this was how my day was going to go I would've never believed you. This is not what I expected when he said he was keeping a secret. "Can I try some of my beautiful fiancé's food," he asks me. I blush but I give him some. He offers me some of his pasta and of course I accept. This food is delicious. Everything just melts in your mouth.

After we eat everything our waiter comes back and ask if we'd like any desert. Donathan smiles at me and tells him we other plans tonight. He hands us our receipt and instructs us to pay at the front. We thank him and he starts to pick up our dishes. Donathan walks around to me and offers me his hand. "My lady," he says. I take his hand and he escorts me to the front.

While I wait for him to pay for our food I stare at my left hand. There is going to be a ring on it shortly. I'm still in shock. We walk outside and he guides me down these extravagant stairs. Reaching the bottom, the valet is already waiting with our car. He opens the door for me, and I get in. He turns around to tip the valet then walks to get in the driver's seat. Putting his hand on the gear shift he turns to me. "Ready love" he asks. I shake my head yes, and we head off to the jewelry store.

Donathan

We arrive to the jewelry store and I park
along the street. Vorie looks over at me and ask,
"Jamie's Jewelers?" I tell her that if we're going to do
this we're going to do this right. We sit in the car for a
couple seconds looking at each other. I did it man. I
really asked this woman to marry me.

I get out of the car and walk around to let her out.
Opening her door, she says, "Are we really doing this
tonight?" I don't dignify that with a response. I offer
her my hand and wait for her to take it. When she's
out of the car I take her hand and kiss it. I hope that's
the yes she wanted.

I walk her into the store, and I'm blinded by the
bright lights inside. These rows of cases each have
their own spotlights. As my eyes adjust a woman
comes over to introduce herself to us. "Hi, welcome.
My name is Edith, would you two like any help this
evening?" she asks. I inform her that we will be
shopping for wedding rings. I can feel it coming out
my mouth, but I can't believe I can hear myself saying

that. I'm wearing a smile so big I know I look like an idiot. She congratulates us and asks when's the big day. Vorie tells her we're actually on way now, and we can see her choke on her words. After we get past the awkwardness in the room Edith leads us over to the wedding ring section of the store. She starts to show Vorie the options that she has and V looks at the tag on each one. I lean over and whisper in her ear, "Stop worrying about the price I'll pay whatever."

Leaving the two women by themselves to browse through rings I walk over to the men's section. I want her to enjoy picking out what she wants without me hovering around. I'm looking for my ring when it really hits me that I'm looking for my ring. In about thirty minutes I'll be able to call Vorie 'Mrs. Ballou'. I glance back at my wife-to-be, and she looks so happy over there looking at the different rings. I don't know why I didn't do this sooner.

I browse my selections some more and I'm leaning toward a clean black band. I love how simple men's rings can be. It makes the decision-making process much easier. I don't care what the ring has on it as long as it means I'm marrying that beauty over there.

I lock in that decision then I walk back over to Vorie and see how things are going.

"I don't know if we should do this," she tells me. My heart shatters inside my chest. This is what I was afraid of. Edith walks away to give us a moment to ourselves. "Babe, what's wrong?" I ask her. She tells me that she doesn't like any of the rings and that must be a sign that this is not right. "I found a ring, so that's a sign that we should do this," I say. Apparently, the wedding isn't about the guy, it's all about the girl, so finding my ring means nothing. She also called me easy to please but I'm going to let it slide because we're crunched for time right now. "How do you know you're looking in the right spot?" I ask her. She questions what do I mean by that, and I remind her that these aren't the only options. "This whole building is filled with prospects, don't limit our future to one section of it," I reason with her.

Taking her hand I led her around the store. I notify her to stop us when she sees something that catches her eye. Walking past one of the last cases she pauses. Pulling us over that way I see it's a selection of classic styled rings. I let her look by herself for a minute before I give any input. I can see that she likes these more, but I still think she's being a little hard on herself. I get behind her and hug her. I feel her small frame melt into my arms. "What do you see Vorie," I ask her. She tells me she doesn't see anything that fits her or what she likes.

I get her to close her eyes and I start massaging her temples. "Take some deep breathes my love," I suggest to her. She starts to calm down and again I ask her what does she see. She bends down to scan the case one more time and her eyes stop once they get to the corner. I wave to Edith and she comes right over. "We've found an option," I express to her. She sees the one Vorie's looking at and unlocks the case. Taking it out she goes to give it to V, but I say, "No, let me."

I take the ring and gently place it on her finger. It goes on like it was made for her. She gasps and puts her hand over her chest, so I already know this is the one. I tell Edith this is definitely the one we're getting tonight.

We walk over to the ring I want so that I can try it on. She takes it out the case and I put it on my finger. The fit is perfect. She tells us since the rings fit so well we can walk out with them right now. As a group, we start to walk to the register and Edith stops. "Did you see the earrings that go with this princess cut band," she asks us. I explain to her we don't need to see them; we'll be getting those too. Vorie tries to reason that she doesn't need them, but I send Edith anyway. As we continue our walk to the register Vorie says, "Babe, why are getting those? They're probably too expensive." I tell her my wife will have the best and nothing less. If it's a matching set, she will have the entire set.

Edith comes to the cash register and begins to box up everything. I swipe my card knowing this might be my largest buy ever. Who cares about a credit card bill when the world's ending though right? Edith hands me everything and we thank her for her help. "I hope everything goes well with your service," she says as we're walking out of the store. Once outside, I give Vorie her earrings. "Change them now while we're in the moonlight," I say. She thinks I'm being dramatic but changes them anyway. The way those earrings shine in her ears look mesmerizing.

"You look stunning sweetheart," I express. I reach into the bag and give her the box with my ring in it. I trust she'll keep it safe until we get to the chapel. I open the door for my lovely fiancé to get in the car. As I'm walking to my side I slide her ring in my pocket. I get in the car feeling like the luckiest man in the world. Reaching for the gear shift, she puts her hand over mine. I look up at her and she says, Let's go do this."

Vorie

We pull up to the chapel and it was packed.
I have never been to a place like this, so I have no
idea what to expect. Donathan takes us around the
back so we can park the car. I'm clinching his ring box
in my hand. We're really here to get married.

Hand in hand we walk around the building to
the front. He opens the door for me and there's a line
of couples almost outside the door. Those skeptical
thoughts I had are starting to come back. "Are we
about to go through with this," I ask. He tells me we
are doing this and for some reason the way he says it
this time brings me comfort. While looking for where
the front desk is Donathan ask me, "Do you think all
these people are here because of the email?" They
could be, but we've only ran into a hand full of people
who have brought it up today. I assumed the majority
of the world was ignoring it.

We find a small open window that was not
visible from the front door and there's a woman,
dressed as a bride, behind it. Her attire is almost

comical until I remember where we are. We get in line and wait our turn to get to the front. While standing here I start to look at all the pictures on the wall of the couples that got married here before today. I wonder if they're even still together. I don't have anything against a chapel like this, but this isn't the type of wedding I dreamed about. I guess I have to remember that time is of the essence.

We get to the front of the line and the bride introduces herself as Gemma. "Have you come to get married tonight or be a spectator?" she asks us. Donathan tells her we've come to be newlyweds, and I can't stop smiling at how giddy he is about this whole thing. She hands us a brochure with many ceremonial options and tells us to pick one. I take the brochure and we step out of line. I'm looking at some of these options and these things are ridiculous. Most of these are too much for us so I suggest we go with the simplest and cheapest option. Donathan agrees with me and we walk back over to pay.

Gemma pencils us in so we have a spot in line and Donathan pays. Before she lets us walk away to get in line she makes sure we both have our rings. I nod my head yes as my grip on the box in my hand tightens. He tells her yes and we walk away. Back in line again there's nothing left for us to do but wait. With each couple that walks through the double doors toward the front I start to think what I will say for my vows. I turn to my left and ask Donathan what he plans on saying for his. "We have to make those up on our own?" he asked and with that I guess I have my answer. I don't even answer his question, I just turn back to the front because I can't with him right now. The woman standing in front of me turns around and ask if I'm nervous. I vigorously shake my head yes and she says, "Oh great, me too." She makes me laugh and in a way starts to ease my nerves. She tells me that her and her boyfriend are here because it's all they can afford. I want to bring up the email, but I don't want to freak her out. She might be hiding their true reason for coming here but that's none of my business.

Our conversation continues until she gets to the front of the line. A worker opens that double doors and ushers for them to come in. She congratulates me on my engagement, and I congratulate her as well.

She grabs my hand and squeezes it. For some odd reason I feel like that is a sign she knows. Once she's gone I'm left to wait until it is I whose turn it is.

We wait for a good fifteen minutes before someone comes back out to call us in. Donathan offers me his hand and we walk through the door together. The first thing I do once we've entered the room is look around. The decorations aren't that bad. There are rows of white pews, pillars on the end of each row, and red carpet covered with white roses. Donathan is walking me down the aisle and *"When A Man Loves A Woman"* by Percy Sledge is playing. We make it to the alter and the moment is finally here. Everything I said before this right here doesn't matter. I'm looking into the eyes of my husband and the decorations, people, nor dress matter. Us and our love makes everything else insignificant.

Our Elvis is dressed in a shiny gold suit. Some things you can't be too picky about. Before he starts he ask us our names. We tell him and he ask one more time are we sure we're ready to do this. Without hesitation and I say yes and Donathan smiles at me. With that he starts our service.

Dearly beloved, we are gathered here today before the sight of God, and in the presence of us to join together this man and woman in Holy Matrimony, which is commended of St. Paul to be honorable estate, instituted of God and therefore is not to be entered into unadvisedly or carelessly, but reverently, joyfully and in the love of God. Into this holy estate these two persons present come now to the joined.

Elvis then ask who gives this bride away for marriage. It's only three of us in here so I don't know who he thought was going to respond. I lift my hand and say I do; that seemed to work enough for him.

Love is patient, love is kind. It does not envy, it does not boast, it is not proud. It is not rude, it is not self-seeking, it is not easily angered, it keeps no record of wrongs. Love does not delight in evil but rejoices with the truth. It always protects, always trusts, always hopes, always perseveres. Love never fails. Donathan and Vorie have come today desiring to be united in this sacred relationship.

He tells us to bow our heads so that he can say a prayer over us. We do as we're told and put our heads down. We say amen in unison then are instructed to join hands. Elvis tells us that now is the time for vows. We could either say some that we have prepared for each other or repeat the ones in front of him. Donathan says he'd like to say his own. Now with how he reacted earlier I'm not expecting some long romantic poem.

Vorie from the moment I saw you I knew I was going to have you. From the first time you smiled at me I knew I'd move mountains and swim oceans to see that mesmerizing smile again. I would say that you complete me but that would be an understatement. You keep me alive, you kickstart my happiness, and you hold the key to my heart in your hands. I don't just want you to be my wife here on earth. I want to feel your love in heaven too. I've grown to realize I must love and cherish the time we have left. I have loved you for better and worse. I've rocked with you when we were rich and when we were poor. In sickness and in health you will not be able to get rid of me. I know we don't have a normal relationship, but you are my best friend. From this second forward I promise to love you harder than the second before. I will never stop choosing you. My wife.

Currently I am speechless. I didn't think he would get up here and make me cry like this. Now I'm thinking that I should've gone first. They're both looking at me because it's my turn and I have to collect myself. Donathan takes my hand to his mouth and kisses it. I have nothing to be worried about.

Donathan Isadore Ballou. You have been my best friend, my home, my kryptonite, and now my husband. The love that we've shared has been like nothing I've ever experienced before. The laughs, memories, and stories we share between us will never grow old and die. You'd mean the world to me if only the world was big enough. I've been by your side until now and I will continue to be in my spot at your side. No love on this earth is stronger than ours and tomorrow I will continue to drown you in my love. I don't know what may come of the time we

*have left but I know I will face it with you
holding my hand.*

I wipe my own tears then I reach up and wipe
Donathan's. Elvis tells us that it is now time to bless
the rings. We both take out the boxes and open them
up. He takes them in his hands and says, "Bless, O
Lord the Giving of these rings that they who wear
them, may live in your peace and your favor all the
days of their life, through Jesus Christ our Lord.
Amen." We each reach into his palm and takes the
other's ring. Putting them on we repeat after him.

*This ring is my sacred gift to you, A
symbol of my Love, A sign that from this day
forward and always, My Love will surround
you, with this ring I thee wed.*

I look at the beautiful ring on my finger and I
think to myself we actually did it. Elvis says, "Let me
reintroduce this couple as Mr. and Mrs. Donathan
Ballou. You may now kiss your wife." Donathan grabs
my face and smashes his lips into mine. We kiss and
he picks me up to twirl around. I have never been
happier than in this moment right here with this man
holding me.

We walk out the back door and we're back in the lobby. With his arm around me we walk outside. "Well now what do we do," I ask Donathan. We make it to the car, and he opens the door for me. "We go on our honeymoon darling," he says as he closes my door.

Donathan

At this time of night there's few places I can take Vorie to celebrate. I'm driving toward the downtown area and I can only think to take her to a club for the night. They'll be dancing, drinks, and I remember it was on our list from earlier. I bring us to a night club I've been hearing about recently at work. It's supposed to be lively on Saturday nights around this time. We arrive and there is no parking. Passing the front of the club, I can already see the line is past the building. I make the block and we have to park several ways down.

I get out and walk around to open the door for my new wife. I don't ever think I'll get used to calling her that. Honestly I don't have the time to but now's not the time to be negative. I offer my hand to help her out and she gives me her left hand. I caught a glimpse of her ring in the moonlight and my knees get weak. My heart skips a beat. Getting her out of the car, I lock the doors and we leave.

We're walking to the club and I can't stop looking at my woman. "Watch where you're going before you fall silly," she tells me. I ignore her and keep making her laugh by staring at the side of her face. We step off the curb and look out for cars as we cross the street. We make it to the other side of the sidewalk, and I don't pick my foot up high enough. I trip and catch myself with my hands before I ruin another pair of pants. I look up and of course she's having a field day with this one. I hate it when she's right. I get up and brush my hands off. If I don't acknowledge it did the fall even happen? I think not.

The line appears to be moving fast so I don't mind standing outside. Vorie's standing in front of me so I wrap my arms around her. "Is this were we're going to be having our first dance," she ask me. I confess I thought that was a question she was supposed to let me ask. She giggles and apologizes. I kiss her on her cheek and tell her, "This is a best place if any to have it. Pretend that everyone is here for us."

We make it to the fourth people in line and the bouncer stops letting people in. He says that the club has reached its capacity for the night. People moan and groan as they start to walk away. "Aww what are we going to do now babe," Vorie ask me. I try to think fast and say what's the harm in going speak to the man.

I walk up to the velvet rope and try to get the guys attention. This huge hulk looking guy comes over and ask what I want. Being assertive I explain to him that Vorie and I just got married and planned for this to be our honeymoon. He looks at me like I'm speaking a foreign language. I'm standing here waiting on a reaction, any reaction. He starts to laugh and ask, "You're bringing your new wife to the club for your honeymoon?" I don't join in his laughter or answer his question, so he starts to settle down. He tells me he can't do anything for me. I take out a $100 bill and slide in into his shirt pocket. "What about now," I ask. He looks at me with a straight face and says, "Yeah.....No." I reach back into my wallet and take out another one. I stuff it in his pocket and raise my eyebrow. He's still not budging. I take out one more bill and give it to him. With both eyebrows raised, he unhooks the rope and says, "Right this way my good man." I grab Vorie's hand and rush into the club before he changes his mind.

Once we get inside I see what he means by reached capacity. We scramble through people packed so tightly there's barely any room to breathe. We make it to the bar, and I secure a seat for my woman. I let her sit down and call over the bartender to get us some drinks. "Are all clubs like this," she whispers in my ear. "Only the good ones," I respond. He comes to us and ask what we want. "A Rum Runner," I say. Vorie's never been to a club before so she ask for a water. We both look at her like a mad woman and I state, "She'll be having a Pina colada." She laughs and tells me she hopes it taste good or I'll be the one drinking it. Little does she know that's exactly why I ordered it.

The music is good tonight. I'm feeling the vibe that's in the atmosphere. Vorie whispers to me that she has to go to the bathroom. I'm a little apprehensive about letting her walk in this packed club alone but she assures me she'll be fine. "Hold down our seat," she tells me as she walks away.

I'm sitting here crowd watching. Looking at all these people enjoying the moment I can't help but wonder what's going to happen to them tomorrow at 7:00 a.m. and do they even know what's in store for us? I decide to take a page out of their book and live in the now rather than stress about what may happen in the morning. From this point forward I refuse to think about the email. I may not be successful, but I make the decision to try. The bartender brings back our drinks and I know he got mine right just based off the color. I take a sip and that warm venom goes down smooth.

I'm halfway through my drink when I realize Vorie has been gone for a long while. I start looking around as if I'm going to see her in this sea of people. I pull out my phone to text her are you ok. As I'm about to press send a hand touches on my shoulder. I turn around in the process of saying, "I'm married" and it's Vorie. "Well I'm happy to know you're not the one I need to worry about," she says. I get out of our seat and let her take it back.

Vorie doesn't drink cocktails much so I try to prepare her for the taste before she takes her first sip.

211

"If it's too strong let me know and I'll have him bring you over a water for real this time," I reason. She takes the first sip and her face lights up. My heart breaks a little. I had plans for that drink. "This is so good Don," she tells me. I fake a smile and shake my head up and down.

I let her finish her little drink before I grab her hand and escort her to the dance floor. All the songs that are currently playing are pretty upbeat. I break out my moves that she hasn't seen before and try to show her what I got. She just ends up laughing at me and telling me to stop. Two songs in and the heat of the dance floor is already unbearable.

We're enjoying the dancing, but this heat is making the floors and walls sweat. A party goer knows that means the body heat in the room is at an all-time high. A slow song finally comes on and everyone grabs their date. I grab my wife because if you didn't know I happen to have one of those now. We're trying our best to try to make this romantic, but people keep bumping into us and I know it's pissing her off. "Would you like to leave V," I bend over and ask her. She nods yes and I take her hand. I'm guiding her through the people, and it's like we're on a jungle excursion. We make it to the door and almost fallen out the club.

When we're outside I make sure she's okay and we have everything before we walk away. I don't want this night to be ruined so I ask her, "Is there anywhere else you would like to go?" She tells me about some poetry slam she saw on our way over here. I didn't see it, so I ask her where it is. "Right around where you fell at," she tells me. I want to say something smart, but I just take my lose. "Lead the way pretty lady," I encourage.

Vorie✒

I lead us back down the street to where I first saw the poetry club. We walk up to the door and from the windows we can see that not a lot of people are here tonight. Perfect. Donathan opens the door and we walk in. There's no one here that seats you when you walk in, so I drag Donathan to a table in the middle of the room.

Up on stage there's an artist doing a piece. I listen and she's spitting some deep stuff. I'm so engulfed in the poem that I don't notice the waiter that comes over and brings us complimentary glasses of water. I take a sip and keep listening. The next artist comes up with their guitar. He plays and delivers his piece at the same time. It was a beautiful moving poem and him adding the guitar on top made it that much better. I wish I could do something like that. I used to come and perform at poetry clubs all the time before Donathan and I started dated. I'm not sure why I stopped. I guess I was just scared of what he'd think of that side of me. I lean over the table a little and ask Donathan how he's enjoying himself.

"This is way more our vibe," he tells me. I'm more than ecstatic that he's showing a liking to this type of thing.

We sit back and watch plenty of other artist grace the stage. Somewhere between artist number seven and twelve I get the courage to go up there. It must have something to do with all the wine and drinks I've been having all day because this isn't like me at all. I sit and form my plan of how to get on stage, but I realize I have nothing on hand to perform. I could freestyle but I've only done that once before. I want to let that stop me but this mysterious courage I have right now isn't letting me tell myself no. I sit and let a couple more artist go before I put my plan into action.

I tell Donathan this water is going straight through me. "You going to the bathroom again? Dang girl," he says. I pay him no mind as I get up and walk toward the bathroom area. I push past the curtain hanging up and make a beeline behind the stage. Like I assumed the host of the night is backstage in the wings. I walk up to him and ask what I have to do to get on stage. He tells me that I can go after the three artist that are already waiting if I want it. I wasn't expecting to go that soon, but I agree to take it, so I won't back out. He ask me what name I would like to be announced under. After short thought I respond, "Mrs. Ballou."

I walk back to our table and take a seat. "I'm really enjoying this more than the club V. Good job spotting this place," he tells me. I express to him I love that he's having a good time. In my head I try to imagine what his face will look like when they call my name. "I wish we would've come to these more," he says. That makes me feel even dumber for keeping my poetry a secret from him for so long. After being with people that find certain things about you boring, you start to keep those things private.

The next artist comes up and that means only two more people before I go up. I don't even know what I'm going to talk about. I don't know what type of battle poet I think I am trying to freestyle up there. The artist finishes and they were okay. The next act flies by and I can't even remember what they talked about. You can tell the house wasn't feeling it and I'm praying that doesn't happen to me.

The last poet before me takes the stage. I can tell from how she's dressed she's about to spit some fire. She starts to talk about being an abandoned body in a world full of nothingness and she has me in the palm of her hands. With each punch line and analogy, she's touching me on a personal level. We're on this walk together and just like that it ends. I stand up to clap and I see that Donathan is standing and clapping with me. When we sit down I ask him did he enjoy that poem. "Yes, I really did," he says. I ask him to go into detail about the things he liked. After giving me a short explanation of what he interpreted from her piece, under my breath I say, "Well, I hope you like mines just as much." He ask me to repeat what I said but before I can open my mouth the announcer is back out again. "Would everyone please give a warmed welcome to our next artist Mrs. Ballou," he says. I look back and Donathan has this look of utter confusion on his face. I get up and I walk toward the stage. I take one step at a time and it feels like my feet alone weigh 100 pounds with each one I take. I get onstage and the announcer gives me the microphone. He walks away and now it's just little old me up here.

> *They say that love thrives on understanding*
> *and trust,*
>
> *I know without a doubt this fact started with us.*

As I perform this poem the whole room fades away. It's me and him. I'm only talking to him.

> *The little things you do,*
> *Show me there's not a soul on earth that could*
> *take the place of you.*
> *You feel like home to me,*
> *Warm and open to one.*
> *Familiar of many things,*
> *A secure and relaxing place.*

He gets up from where we were seated and walks to the bottom of the stage.

> *With your easy smile and knowing touch,*
> *I can't think of another place I love so much.*
> *You're the reason I melt inside,*
> *I pinch myself knowing you're for me.*
> *Through each season in more ways than one,*
> *You show me the importance of growth.*
> *You're the reason my soul happily sings,*

You are more than the real thing.

You're my friend, my lover, and my life,

I declare you the reason my life feels so right.

By the time I'm at the end of my poem I have walked down to the bottom of the stairs. His arms wrap around me and I fall into them. He starts to kiss me, and I can hear a faint sound of cheering around us. "Why didn't you ever tell me you wrote poetry," he asks me. I confess I never thought he'd be interested in that. "I was scared but fear is no longer a factor anymore," I say. He gives me one last kiss on the cheek and says, "I would've been a fool not to love it."

We walk back to our seats and the few people that are sitting next to us tell me I did an awesome job. I thank them and desperately reach for my water. I down the rest in my glass and as if on que the waiter brings me over a fresh glass. I down that one too. I guess I didn't realize how dry my throat got up there. We watch some more artist because I honestly don't want to leave this place.

After a couple more performers the announcer comes back to say they have closed out the poetry section of the night. I get ready to tell Donathan we can leave when he says, "It's time to move into the singers we have coming out tonight." Now this is something I didn't expect. This place keeps getting better and better. The first artist comes out and says she'll be performing an original song. I find myself giddy over this girl and I don't even know if she can sing yet. She begins her ballad and it immediately I'm disappointed. "I wish I had the confidence to sing like that," I tell Donathan. He grabs my hand and says well let's go do it then. I thought he was trying to bring me toward the stage, but he guides me toward the exit. "Where are you taking me," I ask him. He tells me our hour is up and we have more things on our list to get done. "I'm taking you to sing girl," he says. I contend if he wants to sing we can do that here, but he insist on bringing me to a place he knows and I can't protest to that.

Donathan

I'm guiding Vorie down the street and she still has no idea where we're going. My girl says she wants to sing so that's what I'll take her to do. I hope I'm remembering this karaoke spot in the right place. "Where is it D," she asks me. I announce it's a little further, I mean I hope so. "What other hidden talents you been hiding from me," I ask her. She blushes and tells me nothing that I need to be worried about. With seven hours left I can't believe I'm still finding new things to love about this woman. She tries to take the spotlight off her and ask me what talents have I been keeping to myself. "You know about all my talents, but you may not have seen me do them full out," I say. She starts begging me to show her something, but I assure her the moments not right.

Before we see it I can hear the music. Thank God this is the right place. We walk up to the door and there are a lot more people than I expected to be here. Walking in we find our way to an empty booth against the wall. On stage now is a group of white

223

girls singing *"Girls Just Want to Have Fun"*. They look like they are having the time of their lives and are past one drink too many. They finish the song and the bar goes crazy.

A waitress comes over and sets menus down on the table. I ask Vorie if she's hungry, but I know with the dinner we had she's going to say no. I was right, and she pushes the menu away. "We never got any wedding cake," I tell her, "let's see what they have." I open the menu and flip to the deserts.
With so many good-looking flavors it's hard for me to decide. I turn the menu over to her and let her pick.

She orders us a Banana Pudding Cake. My mouth starts watering hearing that name come out her mouth. "You know that's my favorite desert dish right," I ask. She tells me she knows and winks at me. Gosh I love this woman.

As we wait for the cake to be made we sit and watch singer after singer go up and belt out popular songs. Some people are awfully terrible, but we know they're doing it to have a good time. Vorie seems to be enjoying herself and that's all I wanted.

The cake comes out and if I wasn't already in love with Vorie I would think this is what true love felt like. It was the perfect shade of yellow, the whipped cream was in beautiful spiral mounds, and the vanilla cookies were placed ever so slightly lining the top. I want to go in the kitchen and give whoever made this a hug. My eyes start to water from the beauty that she has placed in front of me. I pull out my wallet and hand her a wad of cash. I didn't count it so I can't say exactly what I gave her, but I know for sure that she deserved it. I would pay 1,000s for this cake.

"Would you like to cut it?" Vorie ask me. It's so delicate and elegant I can't even bring myself to so I let her be the one to cut it. She places the first slice on a plate and gives it to me. It takes everything in me to wait until she cuts one for herself. I pick up a fork and I wait for the okay. She nods at me to go and I take the first bite with the swiftness. When the cake hits my mouth it's like an explosion of flavors. I taste banana pudding and vanilla cake. I feel my eyes start to roll back in my head and I have to remember where I am. There should be no one desert that taste this good. "This is amazing," Vorie says. I go to say something, but my mouth is full of cake, so I nod in agreement.

I finish the first slice in record time. My hand immediately goes to cut another slice. Vorie tells me to slow down before I get sick and I quite frankly am insulted. I could never get sick of this adorable golden goodness. I cut two more slices because I already know one more isn't going to do it for me. I start to hear the music around us again and I had no idea that I was blocking it out in the first place. This cake is doing things to me. In the time it takes me to finish three slices Vorie is still working on her one. I decide to pay attention to the singers and give her a chance to enjoy her cake in peace. The guy on stage right now is singing some love song that I'm pretty sure I've never heard before. He's not bad but I know I could do better. I haven't sung in years, but I know I still have the same old pipes. He looks like he's singing to the woman on the front row. That must be his girlfriend or something. I wish I had the courage to sing to Vorie like that. I look back at her and she has some whipped cream on her cheek. I take my thumb and wipe it off for her. When she looks up at me my heart swells. If she can overcome her fear and share her love for poetry with me then I can man up and fully share my talent with her.

I need a little confidence, so I cut myself another piece of cake. Finishing my new slice, I don't feel any better about this then I did before. The waiter comes back over and ask would we like anything else. I order a shot. I know that'll do more good for me. She brings the shot back and I down that quickly. Vorie asks me, "Are you okay?" I ensure her not to worry about me and that I'm fine.

How am I going to sneak away from this table? I don't want to lie to her, but I also want this to be a surprise. "Don, I'm a little thirsty," she tells me. This is my window. I happily agree to go get her a glass of water. Getting up, I walk over to the sign up table. I know she won't see me because her back is turned to the stage.

I get to the front of the line. "What's your name and what would you like to sing," the person sitting ask me. I give my name and that I'd be singing *"Say You Won't Let Go"* by James Arthur. That's the only song I know from front to back that I'm confident in pulling off. He marks my name down and tells me there's two people in front of me. I go past him and check out the backstage area. From here I can see Vorie sitting in our booth eating another piece of cake. My alcoholic courage is kicking in, but I still can feel my hands shaking as I look through these curtains. I watch her as the two singers in front of me go. I can't stop thinking about what she'll think or say. I know she notices I've been gone awhile, because I watch her as she goes to the bar to get her own glass of water.

I feel a tap on the shoulder and it's the host of tonight telling me that I'm up next. I follow him over to the stage and he tells me to wait in the wings. I watch as he goes on stage and tell a few jokes to get the crowd fired up. "And introducing our next singer of the night, Donathan Ballou," he yells. I come out on stage and shake his hand. Taking the mic, I soak in that it's just me out here. I look out into the audience and Vorie is standing by our booth looking at the stage. She looks so confused on why I'm up here. I take a deep breath and the song begins.

Vorieʃ

I hear the announcer say Donathan Ballou, but it doesn't acquire to me that he's speaking of *my* Donathan Ballou. I turn around and he is standing on the stage. I'm confused about what is going on. He tells me he's going get me a water, and now he's on stage. I know that he used to sing but I've never heard him do it seriously. The song starts and the melody sounds a bit familiar.

I met you in the dark

You li t me up

You made me feel as though

I was enough

Those words sound so familiar to me, but I can't exactly place where they're coming from. I know that I've heard this song but it's not hitting me. Donathan sounds amazing.

I knew I needed you

But I never showed

I want to stay with you

Until we're gray and old

When I hear "*Say You Won't Let Go*" I know exactly where this song is from. The night Donathan asked me out we were walking through the park and a street artist was performing this song. We've called it our song ever since. Now I can feel my eyes start to water. This man is standing in front of a room full of people singing his heart out to me. Singing our song to me.

The whole time he's singing he's looking at me and only me. I feel like no one else in this room matters right now. I take a few steps closer to the stage. I watch him as he gives the room one of the most passionate performances I've ever seen. I find myself gravitating closer to the stage as he keeps singing.

> *I want to live with you*
> *Even when we're ghosts*
> *You were always there for me*
> *When I needed you most*

That line hits me different when I think about what may happen in a couple of hours. No one knows if we'll have any memory in heaven. What if we go up together and I don't remember who he is?

I'm going to love you til

Your lungs give out

That line is the one that breaks me. I start to full on cry standing right in front of the stage. In the middle of his singing he motions for me to come closer. I walk up so far my hands can touch the stage. He bends down and wipes my tears. I smile and close my eyes when I feel him brush my cheek. I stay in this same spot and wait until he finishes the whole song. When he's done the whole building goes crazy. He was by far the best singer that graced the stage tonight. Bowing he gives the host back the microphone. I wait for him to come from backstage.

He comes over to where I am and gives me a hug. "I was so nervous," he whispers in my ear. We walk back over to our both and slide in. "You had nothing to worry about sweetie. You are the best singer in here," I inform him. I can't believe that he sounded so astounding and I had no idea. "Why have you never sung full out for me before," I ask him. He says the same reason I didn't tell him I could perform poetry. Touché.

I spend minutes complimenting on his abilities, and I can see him start to blush. I ask him if we wouldn't have come here tonight would he have ever sung for me seriously. "I planned on singing to you at our wedding reception. Well before all this happened. I mean this still sort of counts right," he tells me. I tell him no matter where he did it, it still would've meant the world to me. I've never had someone open up and conquer their fears for me.

I cut us both another piece of cake because this beautiful thing cannot go to waste. We sit here and enjoy the other singers that have come after him. They sound good but nobody sounds better than my man. I get up and walk over to the bar to get two shots. I carry them back over to the table and Donathan helps me set them down. "What are these for?" he ask me. I declare we toast to marriage and life. We tap glasses and throw them back.

"Come up there and sing with me," I hear Don say. I'm looking around trying to find who he's talking to. "You girl! I know you hear me," he says. I laugh it off because I know Donathan isn't asking me to sing a song with him. "Come on baby girl, it'll be fun," he

says trying to entice me. I look at him for a minute
because I must be hearing him speak in another
language. "No," I reply. Grabbing the glasses, I get up
to bring them back to the bar. When I turn around he
is right behind me, and I jump almost knocking down
a bar stool. "What the heck is wrong with you?" I ask
him. He starts begging me to come on a stage and sing
with him. "I know you're scared. I am too but let's do
it to say we've done it." he tells me. The more I think
about it the more he's right. Now's not the time to be
holding back because I'm scared. Now's the time to
run full steam ahead.

I break down and agree to go on stage with
him. "I'm only singing one song and I hope you know
that," I inform him. He tells me one song is all he
needs. He takes my hand and drags me over to the
sign-up table next to the stage. "Coming to grace us
again, Mr. Ballou," the man behind the table ask. The
guy sings one time and they already know his name.
Donathan looks at me and ask what song I would like
to sing. I have no ideas off the top of my head, so I
look at the list under the duet's column. The first song
I see I notice is *You Are the Reason* by Calum Scott

and Leona Lewis. Without much thought I pick that song for us. He agrees and the guy writes it down. We move backstage and my nerves get to kicking in high gear. We have only one person in front of us so if I want to bail I better make up my mind fast. Donathan grabs my hand and tries to calm me down. I hate that he knows me so well sometimes. Okay that was a lie. "What if I suck?" I ask him. He tells me it's not about being good it's about having fun. That sounds very corny, but I try to take that advice seriously.

The singer before us is coming from off the stage so I know that means we're next. Donathan starts to walk away but my feet feel like they're stuck in one place. I say a quick prayer, so God won't let me embarrass myself. I force my feet to follow him to the wings of the stage. "Welcome back to the stage everyone's favorite of the night and his wife. Donathan and Vorie Ballou," the host announces. We walk out and there are already two microphones set up on stage for us. I take the one closest to the exit in case this doesn't work out. The screen in front of us says the name of the song and music starts to play. I couldn't be happier that I picked a song where he goes first. I don't know if I would've had the courage to start the song.

I'm gripping this mic like a snake wrapped around its prey. My part is coming up and I'm shaking so much I think I'm shaking the screen. Donathan reaches over to grab my hand, and I take a deep breath.

From the time I open my mouths to the end of the song I keep my eyes on him. We make eye contact the whole time and it feels like we're together alone in our living room. I focus only on him and by the end of the song I don't even realize we're at the end. The audience claps and it snaps me out of my trance. He takes my hand and guides me off stage. When we get in the wings I'm still in shock. He hugs me and says, "Baby you did it. You sounded great." I was concentrating on him so much that I didn't even hear what I sounded like. We come from backstage and the people start to clap all over again. As we walk to our booth I wave and say a bunch of thanks. "That was kind of fun," I tell him. At least I think it was. We laugh and I finish the rest of my glass of water I left.

"We only have a few hours left love, what's left to do?" he asks me. I take the list out and find one thing I can't leave this earth without us doing. "A dance on the beach," I admit. He looks at me like I must be crazy. "You want to go dance on the beach at one in the morning?" he asks me. I assure him I definitely do. Getting up, I hold my hand out for him to take. He huffs but gets up and grabs it.

Donathan

I open the door to the karaoke bar, and we walk outside. She wants to go to the beach from here, but I don't even think I remember how to get to the boardwalk. Holding hands, I guide her in the direction I think it is and hope for the best.

I'm starting to hear the waves crashing and I know we can't be that far. "Do you know where you're going?" Vorie ask me. I comeback with of course I do and keep walking. Right when I start to doubt myself I see the sign for the boardwalk. "See woman, I told you I knew what I was doing," I state. God is always looking out.

We get to the actual boardwalk and it looks beautiful tonight. The lighting is marvelous, the breeze is perfect, and there's no one else out here. We casually walk down the boardwalk not saying anything to each other. Just taking in the beauty of tonight.

"What do you think heavens going to be like?" Vorie ask me. I tell her I honestly don't know. I want to believe it looks like this but perfect. I hope the streets are golden. I'm pretty sure everything up there will be white and gold. I mean it's only right. I wonder if there's going to be a sky up there or will it be endless whiteness. It would be dope if we had cars up there. Wait that wouldn't make sense because we'll have wings anyway (scratch the car thing). After pulling myself out my thoughts I ask Vorie what she thinks it'll be like. "We'll each get our own house. It'll be everything we've ever wanted. I don't think I'll forget about you. It seems silly for God to go through the trouble of creating someone just for me to have me forget them so easily. I don't think we'll know anybody else though," she tells me. Her version of heaven doesn't sound too bad, but like mine a little more.

Now that she's brought up this topic my mind is swirling with questions. The main one bugging me is what will he look like. Everyone has their own opinion of what they think he looks like, but I know we're all wrong. Will I see him and already know that's him? I think I will. He'll walk with so much authority I'll have no choice but to know. Does God even walk, or does he just float everywhere? Well if they can send emails from up there I doubt anything isn't possible.

"Do you think it'll hurt when he comes," she ask me. I respond no but I'm not so sure of that answer. Will the sky open up and we'll evaporate? Will our souls just leave our bodies at the same time? Will a VIP escalator just shoot down from the sky? All these thoughts are making my head throb.

We've been walking on this boardwalk for a while now. There still isn't a soul in sight. I take Vorie's hand and I start to spin her around. She laughs and tells me to slow down some. The way her ring is glistening right now makes my stomach drop. "We have to go down to the water for this dance to count," she tells me. We make our way to the stairway that leads to the sand below. I pick her up and begin to carry her down the stairs. "Normally it would be a threshold, but this will have to do for now," I say. Once at the bottom I place her on her feet. We both bend down to take our shoes off. "Let's leave them here by the stairs, nobodies out here," she tells me. I do as she says and place our shoes under the stairs.

I take her hand and we begin to walk toward the water. I hate the feeling of my toes on this sticky sand. "I want to get my feet wet first V," I express. I let go of her hand and run for the water. I can hear the sound of her feet as she follows me. The water touches my feet and sends chills down my spine. The water is cold tonight. It's so clear tonight it looks as if its sparkling. I don't bother to roll my pants legs up; I just keep on walking. Vorie doesn't follow me at first but I walk until I am waist deep in this ocean. I stand here and look up at the sky. Why me? Why us? Why right now?

Vorie places her hand on my shoulder. I turn around and she's completely in the water with her dress still on. I hug her very close to me knowing she doesn't know how to swim. This girl is asking to be taken early. We stand in the water for a while with me holding her. For some reason time feels like it stands still when you're in water. It flows around us while everything else stands unchanged.

When my arms get tired I start to carry Vorie back toward the shore. I put her down where I know she can walk. She starts to walk away from me, and I brush my hand across the top of the water throwing some her way. It hits her hair and I know that was a mistake. "Did you get my hair wet," she yells at me. Trying my luck, I respond, "No." Now this only infuriates her more. She scoops up as much water with her hands as she can and throws it at my face. I dodge it and immediately I regret it. She comes charging at me through the water. I start to back up, but I stop. I know she'll come after me even though it'll kill her to. I wait until she gets close to me and wrap my arms around her. She squirms in my arms and I say, "If you don't stop moving I'm going to dip your whole head in." She stops. "You wouldn't dare," she tells me. I dare her to try me and find out. Her body relaxes against my arms. I let her go and she takes a step back. I start walking back toward the sand. I thought I was in the clear until I felt something dripping down my neck. I reach to the back of my neck and feel water. I turn around and she's looking around, water dripping from her hands. If she wants to play dirty so can I. I rush over to her and swoop her up before she can even move. She yelps in surprise not expecting me to make it to her so fast. "Don't you dare," she says to me. I look her in the eyes, stiffen my body, and fall back into the water.

The water consumes us. I feel her thrashing around, and I get up on my feet to pick her up out the water. Placing her on her feet she starts wiping the water from her eyes. Flipping her hair back she stares at me. I expect her to be very upset but to my amazement she starts laughing. I can't keep up with this woman. I walk over to her and I kiss her. I can't resist a moment to feel her lips. "We have to go have our dance now," she tells me. We walk through the water making it back to the sand. "Let's do it right here," she tells me. I look at the spot she's showing me and I'm not feeling it at all. If we are going to do this it has to be perfect and I will make it perfect. "No baby we have to find the perfect spot," I plead. She makes this face and I know in her mind she's calling me dramatic. Without saying a word, she starts to walk down the beach. I run up behind her and throw her over my shoulder. "What in the world are you doing," she says trying not to laugh. I spin in circles and she can't contain herself. I put her down and she stumbles some. I guess I made her a little dizzy. She grabs my hand to steady herself and we start to make our way down the beach.

Vrie

He makes me walk for what feels like ten minutes. I don't know what's up with his obsession to make our dance perfect, but my feet can only take so much longer. I go to open my mouth and tell him, but he stops anyway. "This is it," he says. That is more than music to my ears.

We stand where he wants, and I wait for him to pull his phone out. The song starts and it's the same one he sung for me at the karaoke bar. "No, no no, you have to pick a new song. That was our song before but now we need a married song," I tell him. I realize that now I'm the one that sounds extra. "You are serious, aren't you?" he asks me. I inform him I'm not dancing until he changes it.

He flips through his songs for a while and I just look at the screen. He moves the phone where I can't see and says, "If I have to pick then you can't know what it is." Men am I right? I let him have his little moment.

I glance around to see why he chose this as our perfect spot. The water looks the same, the sand isn't any cleaner, and I'm pretty sure the temperature feels the same down here too. I think he's pulling my leg on this one.

I look up and it looks as if the moon is shining right where we are standing. It's sort of our spotlight. He wasn't searching for the perfect spot; we were chasing the moonlight. *Oh, he's good.*

He starts the song and a soft piano begins. "What song is this," I ask him. He tells me it's one that makes him think of me. I don't ask him any further questions. I take his outstretched hand and lay my head on his chest. We don't say anything and just let the lyrics cloth us in the moment.

For all we know

We may never meet again

Before you go

Make this moment sweet again

I've never heard this song before, but I can feel it tugging at my heart strings already. We sway back and forth to the music and the sound of the waves.

For all we know

This may only be a dream
We come and we go
Like the ripples of a stream

I let him pick a song and he picks the only love song I've ever heard in the world about tomorrow possibly not coming. Sometimes I understand this man and other times I can't fathom why he chooses to do the things he does. I'm sobbing, not holding myself together at all. There's no hiding my ugly crying so I don't even try to. The song is awfully short, so it ends abruptly. "Put it on repeat," I say. He picks the phone up and does as he's told. I take him back in my arms and I cry. I don't try and stop it; I know it needs to come out. Holding him I feel something slide down my shoulder. I look up and he's crying too. I wipe his tears and put my face back against his chest.

We dance to this song on repeat at least thirty times. "Are you tired hun?" he asks me. I told him no. He cuts the song back on and we continue to dance. It feels like as long as this song is on we are safe. He takes my hand and starts to spin me around. He knows that makes me smile. He twirls me into him and dips me down. It catches me off guard. I put my hand on his chest to stabilize myself. He bends down to kiss me. We start to dance around, and my feet in the water again. We dance at the water's edge and this honestly feels like a fairy tale to me. The man I love sweeping me off my feet under the moonlight on the beach. If it's not already somebodies' story they need to make it one.

I feel myself get tired and I know that means I can't keep up much longer. I wish we could stay up through the night and be with each other, but I can't push myself any longer. "I'm tired Don," I say. We walk back over to his phone and he picks it up. Stopping the music, he tells me, "Let's go home." I love our home but that's not where I want to spend my last night here. "There's one last thing I want to do before we call it quits," I confess. I take out the list and hand it over to him. "Sleep under the stars?," he ask me, and I shake my head yes. He smiles at me and agrees with my last request. Not wanting to sleep out in the open he tells me we have to find the right spot to sleep in. "That's fine but I'm not walking this whole beach Donathan," I inform him. He pays me no mind and grabs my hand.

We walk until we come across this cave-like area. It's very dark and I'm skeptical about going in there. "You go check it out first," I tell him. He tries to assure me it's safe but I'm not moving an inch until he sees what's inside first. He rolls his eyes at me but begins to walk in the cave. I see him disappear in the darkness and for some reason my heart starts to beat very fast. For the first time today, I'm by myself and it doesn't feel right. Seeing him walk into that dark abyss makes me feel like he's gone. I call out to him and at first, he doesn't come back right away. I'm scared shitless but I don't have the courage to go after him by myself. I see a small spec that starts to enlarge, and I know it's him. He walks back over to meet me, and I throw my arms around him. "I was only gone two seconds V," he tells me. I ignore him and wait for my heartbeat to slow down. He confirms that the cave is clear but after just now I'm too terrified to go fully in. "Can we stay closer to the outside, so I can see the stars," I ask. He tells me yes and we start to walk to the cave.

We get to the opening and I can feel my body starting to shut down. Taking a seat on the sand I give my feet a break. Donathan lays down beside me and I let my body fall back into his arms. My eyes are already closed before I can even snuggle up next to him. I reposition myself to get comfortable and he tells me to open my eyes. I do and the sky is filled with shooting stars. "This is incredible," I say. They're lighting up the sky and it's unlike anything I've ever seen before. "You know shooting stars mean positivity," he tells me. I say I sure hope so and my eyes start to get heavy again. "I love you Donathan," I express. He tells me he loves me even more and I nestle my head in the crook of his neck. I request that he watch the sunrise in the morning with me. I know it'll be cutting it close, but I'd love to see it one last time. He sets an alarm on his phone for 6:30 a.m. and I give into the sleep I've been fighting.

Donathan

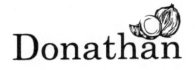

I look over at her as she's sleeping. She looks so peaceful when she's like this. I check my phone to see how much time we have. It's not that far from when she wanted me to wake her up. I can't bring myself to get her up any earlier. If I could let her sleep until it's time I would do that. I don't know if this is going to hurt so I'd rather her go in her sleep. That's one of the more peaceful deaths. That can't hurt, could it? I mean you're asleep.

I can't spend any second longer thinking about this stuff. After she went to sleep early this morning I let my mind get the best of me and now it's almost 6:30 a.m.. I couldn't go to sleep feeling as helpless as I do. In a last stitch effort, I try and persuade God one last time.

Dear God,

We are sorry for the things that we've done. I don't know what else we can do to show you that we're sorry other than to change our behavior. If you would please find it in your heart to give us

one last chance to show you we can do better, I
promise we would. You could even give us a
trial period and see how we do. Two months?
Three months? Or even six months? However
long you think we need but please don't shut us
down today. Please don't take this girl away
from me. I've served you well, but I can admit
that I'm not the most perfect Christian. If you
could find it in any way to change your plans
for today I ask that you please do.

Amen,

Your Son – Donathan

I'm not sure my prayer will do anything, but it
made me feel better in the slightest. She starts to
move against my body, and I know that means she's
waking up. I watch as she wrinkles her nose and tries
to open her eyes fully.

She wakes and the first thing she looks at is
me. "Good morning sleepy head," I say. Continuing to
adjust she ask me how long I have been watching her.
I tell her I haven't been to sleep yet, and she can't
believe me. She gets up from the sand and starts to
stretch out her back. I guess sleeping on the beach

wasn't as cute as we thought it would be. While she's yawning I ask her how did she sleep. "As best as I could under the circumstances," she tells me. She ask me why I didn't go to sleep and honestly I couldn't take my eyes off her. I mention that and she looks at me with loving eyes. "You're going to be sleepy later," she tells me, and I know she didn't catch what she said. I don't say anything because I don't want to hurt her feelings.

Without me having to say anything, I can see from her body language that she remembers what today is. I come over and hug her from behind. "It's okay babe, you forgot. It happens," I express. She shakes her head at me, but I don't think she's taking what I'm saying seriously. "How dumb must I be to forget the end of the world," she tells me. I don't know what to do when she says things like that about herself. I try to relief the situation and ask if she would like to do anything else with the short time we have left. She tells me she has no energy to do anything else but watch the sunrise. Offering her my hand I state, "Well let's go find your dream spot." She takes it and we start to walk out of the cave.

When we get out in the open it's actually still dark outside. I've never watched the sun come up before, so I don't know how much time we have. I let her take the lead on this one because I know this is the one thing she wants in the world that I can't give to her. I let her lead me all over the beach until we find a spot that she feels is perfect. "What do you think of right here," she asks me. I respond if she likes it then the spot is impeccable. I sit down first and make a spot for her between my legs. She sits down and leans back against me. "I wish we would've brought some breakfast with us, but I won't even get to enjoy it before it's time," she tells me. I laugh a little to lighten the mood but if I'm honest I'm hungry too. I look around us and notice there are palm trees not that far away. It's a long shot, but I request that she wait right here for a minute.

I get up and start walking over to the palm trees. I can't see from this far if they have brown circles under the leaves, but I shoot up a quick request to God. "If you got my prayer this morning please let there be coconuts on this tree," I say aloud.

Fingers crossed I approach the tree with my eyes closed. I wait until I can stick my hands out and touch the trunk before I look up. I knew God could hear us up there. There are two coconuts sitting at the top of the tree tucked underneath a group of leaves. Part 1 of my plan is going pretty smoothly. I've never tried climbing a tree before and I don't plan on learning at this very second. "What are you doing," I hear off in the distance. I pay her no mind and focus on how I'm going to get our breakfast out of this tree. I've seen people just shake the tree and they've fallen out, but I've only ever seen that in movies. I doubt it could work but it couldn't hurt to give it a try. I give the trunk a shake and the coconuts come rolling down stopping at my feet. You've got to be kidding me.

I pick up the two coconuts and bring them back over to where Vorie is. "What the heck are those," she asks me. I had an inappropriate joke in my head at the time but with the ending of the world, I didn't feel it fit the mood. I pick up a huge rock from the water and bring it over. She's looking at me like I'm an idiot, but I'm about to blow her mind. I slam the rock on the coconut, and nothing happens. The movies sure made

257

this look easy. She coughs under her breath and looks away from me. I know she's hiding a laugh, but I don't let that discourage me.

I continue to slam this rock on the coconut until it gives way and cracks open. In my mind juice was supposed to go everywhere but that didn't happen. I pick up the fruit and peel back the part that has cracked open. Nobody told me that the actual coconut is inside the coconut! I am pissed at every movie that made it look so simple. I want to give up, but I've come too far to let this coconut win. I peel all the outer layer off so I can get to the goodness on the inside. I take it and slam it against the sand, and it opens with ease. That's what was supposed to happen the first time.

I hand her the part of the fruit that holds the water. She takes in her hands and looks at me like she's amazed at what I did. "You didn't know your man was a survivalist did you," I state proudly. She laughs at me as she starts to drink the water from the coconut.

I let her eat while I start the process all over again. Once I get my coconut open I take a seat next to her. The water isn't as sweet as I thought but it tastes better than an empty stomach.

I'm halfway done with my fruit when I decide to end the silence between us. "What was your favorite part of the day," I ask her. She tells me watching me fly in the air off of a horse had to be the highlight of her day. Her answer makes me choke on my water. I look over at her and she is having the laugh of a lifetime. "That's cold V," I say. She returns my question and I respond that sky diving had to be the highlight of my day. Feeling that free and experiencing something I never would've done if not for that email felt satisfying.

"Yesterday was the best day of my life sweetheart," she tells me. I assure her it was no big deal, but she insists on thanking me. "I didn't do this alone V. You made yesterday the best day for me too," I reassure her. She smiles to herself as she eats pieces of the coconut.

The sun starts to peer its head from the ocean's end. We turn our full attention to the beauty that's unfolding before us. It's hard to believe this happens each morning and this is my first time seeing it. We sit on the sand frozen still watching the colors consume the dark blue sky. Somehow my hand finds hers and holds onto it. It starts to hit me that with or without us this earth moves on. Each morning the sun comes up and each night the moon rules the sky and they don't need us to do it. This is showing me how mighty nature is and insignificant the power we have is.

I glance down at my phone and see that it's 6:55 a.m., which causes my heart to drop and chills run over my body. I don't want to tell her, because I don't want to ruin her moment. I go to call her name and before I can say it, she tells me she can already feel it's time. Standing up, she picks her head up to the sky. With her arms outstretched I put myself between them. With my head on her shoulder, for the first time since this all started I speak out loud that I'm terrified. She tells me I have nothing to be afraid of because I'm not facing this alone. I hug her even tighten then before.

At this point, I'm shaking thinking of the seconds counting down. I resort to the only thing I know how to do and ask Vorie to pray with me one last time. I ask him for forgiveness for anything that

260

I've ever done that dishonors him. I pray for the protection of both of our spirits. I ask him to shower us with love and overflow us with calmness. My mind is all over the place and I don't know what else to say, so I end the prayer with an amen. She says it after me and we stand with our foreheads touching for a few seconds more.

I take one more look at my phone and it reads 6:59 a.m. I show her, and I can see her eyes swell up with tears. "I want to hear our song one last time," she pleads to me. As quickly as I can, I turn our song on for her. It starts and I watch the clock as it turns to 7:00 a.m. On instinct, I throw my arms around her and hold her close.

Immediately the sun starts to shine brighter. My grip on her starts to tighten. As seconds pass the light gets too bright for me to hold my eyes open anymore. I squeeze them shut and call out I love you one last time hoping she can hear it. I can feel her body in my arms diminish. I try to tighten my grip on her, but my arms fall against my own body. I'm crying and scrambling my arms around reaching for something to cling to. My arms come up empty. I can feel myself trembling, but I can't bring myself to open my eyes. I put my hands over my face and drop to my knees. It feels like I'm in the middle of a tornado the way the air is passing around me. My fear magnifies and I begin to shake not knowing what is happening around me.

The sounds stop and I can feel I'm not moving anymore. With my hands still over my eyes, I keep at my knees with my head buried in my lap. An unfamiliar voice in a soft whisper tells me it's okay to open my eyes now. For reasons unknown I trust in this voice and slowly remove my hands from my eyes. Standing up I find myself face to face with a picket that is larger than anything I've ever seen. I stumble back and see that it's a small part to the golden fence that seems to go on for miles. I look around and I'm alone. Cautiously I go up to the gate and press on it. It doesn't open for me. I see a figure through the gate, and I call out to them. They hear my cries and begin to turn around. I can't tell what this figure is from this far away. As it moves closer, my eyes begin to adjust to all the white. I have to rub my eyes a little because I don't think I'm seeing what's in front of me right. I can't be. Once they are in arms reach I see that I'm not crazy. It's …Vorie.

Epilogue:

Donathan

I jump out of bed in a cold sweat. I've been having the same dream about Vorie for the past week now and it feels so real to me. It starts with us getting this alarming email claiming God is shutting the world down. We came up with the plan to spend our last hours doing things off our couples' bucket list.

When I look over at the clock, I realize it's only eight o'clock. I can't bring myself to get out of bed and go to this funeral today. Since Vorie's car accident and death a week ago this bed has been the only place for me to go. All I can seem to think about is the time we've lost. If God would've given me a day's notice, I would've made our last day together the best one possible. I get out of bed and head to the kitchen to get a drink. Opening the fridge I see she's left me a note that we need to go to the grocery store. I haven't touched that note since she left it for me. I can't bring myself to take it down. It's the last thing I have from her. That morning a little over a week ago I didn't get to tell her bye like I usually do. I overslept because I was so tired, and she let me get my rest. I didn't get to kiss her and wish her a good day or ask her what were we going to eat for dinner that night. Our last encounter is this note. I reach around it and grab the pitcher of orange juice. I pour myself a glass, position the carton back behind her note, and go get back in bed.

I'm laying here staring at the ceiling, and it feels like I'm living in a simulation. I've been dreading today and seeing that it's here I don't even want to get dressed. If I get up and put on clothes it makes everything all real. I stretch my arm out and the spot next to me is empty. I don't think I'll ever get used to this feeling.

I man up and get up because regardless of what I want this day will move on without me. Walking into our closet it's hard to pass by her clothes. I turn my back to them and look at what my options are. I could wear my black suit to reflect what I'm feeling on the inside, but I don't want that to be my reasoning. She means more to me then coping out like that. I decide to put on my gray suit. I know she always loved to see me in gray.

I carry the suit out of the closet and lay it out on the bed. I go into the bathroom and start the shower. Getting in I can feel the water's too hot, but my body is too numb to do anything about it. I get clean and quickly get out. I reach for my clean towel on the counter and I catch a glimpse of myself. I don't look like me, I look like a shell of who I used to be. The brownness in my skin is dull and the light that was once in my eyes is gone. I don't even recognize the man standing before me. I continue to dry off and walk back into my room. As I start to get dressed I feel like I'm moving in slow motion. Buttoning my shirt, it'll take me forever to get to the top.

I walk back into the closet to pick out a tie and some shoes. Vorie usually did this for me, I'm not good at putting colors together. I stick with black and play it safe. I go in my watch drawer and pick up the first one my hand touches. Checking the time, I see I have to leave soon if I want to make it on time. I bring my empty glass of orange juice back to the kitchen sink. Feeling the need for a pick me up I reach into my

267

lucky cabinet and pull out my bottle of whiskey. Taking a shot glass, I pour myself one. Throwing it back I can feel the warm sensation going down my body. It's the only other thing I've been able to feel other than overwhelming sadness. I pour another and quickly down it. I grab my keys and wallet heading for the door. On the way out I slide the folded piece of paper sitting on the counter in my jacket pocket.

I get on the elevator and take it down to the parking garage. I haven't even thought about driving a car since Vorie's accident. The doors open and my feet don't move. My legs don't start moving until someone else gets onto the elevator. It feels as if I'm floating to the car. I get to the door and scramble to get the keys out of my pocket. I pull them out and they slip right through my fingers. Bending over to pick them up I hit my head against the car door. I pick up the keys and take a deep breath. I haven't even gotten there yet and I'm already falling apart. Unlocking the car door, I take a moment to sit there and collect myself. Never in life would I have thought this would be something I had to face alone.

Hearing the roar of the car come to life makes my heart race. I would drive this car every day and getting into an accident is never the first thing on my mind. Until now. I'm terrified to put this thing in drive. Now wrecking is all I can think about. I rub the pocket of my jacket and try to calm myself down. It's no possible way I'm missing today so I am going to have to pull myself together. I build the courage to pull out of the parking garage. Cruising into the slow lane my foot won't push the gas down faster than 40 mph and it's not bothering me. I could take this route in my sleep. It feels like my hands are possessed and they control the wheel. Every red car that passes me reminds me of her. Wonder how long that will last.

Pulling up to the church I can already see there is a lot of people outside. My nerves get shot and my hands begin to shake. I have no idea how I'm going to get through this. My brain starts to spiral in all possibilities of how this could go bad. I have to stop myself. What am I doing? I'm going to get out of this car, I will go inside this church, and I will get myself together. This wasn't just some girl to me. This was the girl I was going to marry, and I will act like it. I give myself five more minutes to collect myself and I get out of the car. I walk toward the grand stairs leading up to the church and my chest starts to get tight. Getting to the front door her mother greets me and says, "All family will be sitting to the front, that includes you." I reply with a simple yes ma'am and continue to walk in the church.

As I'm walking in people from all sides are trying to get my attention. The only words I can make out are sorry for your loss. I keep replying thank you every which way I hear a voice. I walk in the sanctuary and it's pretty empty at the moment. I get to the middle aisle, and I see that light pink casket resting at the front of the church. My knees instantly get weak. My legs carry me down the aisle. My mind starts to short circuit. She was supposed to be the one meeting me at the altar not the other way around. I make it to the front and my heart feels like it could rip my chest open. My love looks stunning. Yellow was always her best color. I place my hand on the side of the casket, but I can't bring myself to touch her. I feel a wetness on my face, and it isn't until now that I realize I'm crying. A tear falls on her cheek and my instinct is to wipe it from her. She feels so cold. This really isn't a dream. I stand over her for a moment just looking at her. It feels real but at the same time, it feels like this isn't happening to me. People start to pile into the church because the service is about to start. I take the ring out my pocket that I've been saving for weeks and place it in there with her. I never got the chance to give it to her, but I hope she can see it now.

I take my seat on the front row next to her mother. She grabs my hand and holds it tight. We wait while the guests come in and pay their respects. From where I'm sitting I can still see her face. My eyes don't leave her for one second. The pastor walks up to the podium and everyone begins to take their final seats. He gives everyone a few seconds before he begins to speak. "Today we have gathered to honor the life of Vorie Elizabeth Adams," he says. I hear him but my mind isn't registering what he's saying.

I can feel the tears falling uncontrollably down my face and her mother puts her arm around me. I fall into her and let everything I've been holding in out. She rubs her hand on my back and I give into it more. Taking the note out of my pocket, I hold it in my hands. Unfolding it, I see her handwriting and it makes my heart jump. This was the list. Our list. I shouldn't have taken our time together for granted. I could've given her the world. I take one last look at her before they come to close the casket. As they bring the top down I can feel the numbness inside of me begin to grow. I lost my everything.

Acknowledgements

First I would like to thank God for giving me the idea for this book. Without him I would not have been able to finish this book at all.

I would like to thank my family for being there to uplift me when I doubted myself in putting this out.

I have to thank my PVAMU family for staying on top of me in releasing my book and showing an interest in wanting to read my story.

Lastly I must thank myself. Thank you for pushing me to write even when I didn't want to. Thank you for editing the cover each time I wanted to change something so small that nobody would even notice. Thank you for praying over me when I needed it the most. If I didn't have you, I would not have the confidence to share this. You did your thing girl.

Authors Favorite Lines

I'd rather be a fool now than be sorry later.

Time isn't measured by clocks, but by the memories you make with the seconds you have.

On earth and in heaven we are bound.

It took some email that I don't even know is real to show me the beauty I wake up to every morning.

If people treated something I made like we do this earth I'd take my gift back too.

I wonder if we look like microscopic germs to him infecting the earth he built for us to cherish.

I got comfortable in winning the girl that I forgot to keep learning my mate.

When you take the time to shut up and listen you can hear the world scream around you.

Instead of helping each other to fix the problem we overlook our neighbor until it's happening to us.

Silly me to think we had all the time in the world.

Don't stray from the storm, learn to sail through it.

Live in the now rather than stress about what may happen tomorrow.

He wasn't searching for the perfect spot, we were chasing the moonlight.

Each morning the sun comes up and each night the moon rules the sky and they don't need us to do it.

Ask yourself if today was your last day on earth would you be satisfied with the life you've lived?

If not choose today to make a change.

Scriptures Of Proof

"Whereas ye know not what *shall be* on the morrow. For what *is* your life? It is even a vapour, that appeareth for a little time, and then vanisheth away."

James 4:14 (KJV)

"Boast not thyself of tomorrow; for thou knowest not what a day may bring forth."

Proverbs 27:1 (KJV)

"Take therefore no thought for the morrow: for the morrow shall take thought for the things of itself. Sufficient unto the day *is* the evil thereof."

Matthew 6:34 (KJV)

"The life of mortals is like grass,
   they flourish like a flower of the field;

the wind blows over it and it is gone,
   and its place remembers it no more."

Psalms 103: 15-16

About The Author

Paris Keal is a young Digital Media Arts major at the illustrious Prairie View A&M University in Prairie View, TX, originally coming from the small town of Port Arthur, TX.

Instagram: @naturallypeh

Facebook: Paris Keal

CPSIA information can be obtained
at www.ICGtesting.com
Printed in the USA
LVHW111035150620
658119LV00001BA/10